SCOUNDREL FOR SALE

A WICKED WIDOWS' LEAGUE BOOK

COURTNEY MCCASKILL

HAZEL GROVE BOOKS

BOOKS IN THE WICKED WIDOWS' LEAGUE SERIES

Book 1: Dawn Brower—Wicked Widows' League
Book 2: Dawn Brower—Her Rogue for One Night
Book 3: Lana Williams—To Bargain with a Rogue
Book 4: Cara Maxwell—Rogue Awakening
Book 5: Ari Thatcher—My Lady Rake
Book 6: Diana Bold—A Scoundrel in Gentleman's Clothing
Book 7: Amanda Mariel—Rogue for the Taking
Book 8: Courtney McCaskill—Scoundrel for Sale
Book 9: Charlie Lane—Scandalizing the Scoundrel – available May 9, 2023
Book 10: Sue London—To Woo a Rake – available May 16, 2023
Book 11: Anna St. Claire—A Widow's Perfect Rogue – available May 23, 2023
Book 12: Rachel Ann Smith—Stealing a Scoundrel's Heart – available May 30, 2023
Book 13: Tracy Sumner—Kiss the Rake Hello – available June 6, 2023
Book 14: Nadine Millard—Seducing the Scoundrel – available June 13, 2023

First published in 2023 by Hazel Grove Books.

Paperback ISBN: 978-1-63915-011-3

Kindle ISBN: 978-1-63915-009-0

eBook ISBN: 978-1-63915-010-6

This is a work of fiction. Names, principal characters, events, and incidents are the products of the author's imagination. A few real historical figures make cameo appearances. The scenes in which these characters appear have no factual basis. Any other resemblance to actual persons, living or dead, or actual events is purely coincidental.

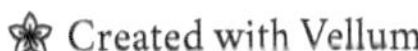 Created with Vellum

PROLOGUE

Salamanca, Spain
July 1812

THE FIRST CATASTROPHE came in the form of a letter.

The second took a more familiar shape, at least for a lieutenant in the King's Own Regiment of Foot.

A bullet.

The bullet didn't strike Gabriel Davenport, although he would've preferred that it did. The reason he would've preferred it was because the person it did strike was Alexander Stapleton, variously known as Viscount Hartlebury to the *ton*, Captain Lord Hartlebury to his troops, and 'Hart' to his friends.

Gabe thought of Hart as more of a brother than a friend.

The annoying thing was that the battle was all but over. Their regiment was driving the retreating French toward the forest when Hart bit out a curse and clutched his thigh.

Gabe hurried to his side. "What is it?"

"Bullet," Hart said through clenched teeth.

"Let me see," Gabe said, prising Hart's fingers from his leg. He thought his friend fortunate at first. The leg was one of the better places to get shot, all things considered.

"Come on," Gabe said, pulling Hart's arm over his shoulder. "Let's get you to the surgeon."

They made it all of ten steps before Gabe noticed that Hart's face was losing its color. He glanced down and started at the bright red stain on his friend's trousers. It was growing so fast, he could see it spread.

After three years in the army, Gabe had a certain amount of experience when it came to bullet wounds.

This one was bleeding like the *dickens*.

"Bloody hell," Gabe said, pulling Hart to a stop. He laid his friend on the ground and began searching inside the satchel where he kept his powder and shot. "That needs a tourniquet."

"G-Gabe," Hart said through clenched teeth.

Gabe kept digging through his satchel. Officers were encouraged to carry a field tourniquet into battle for precisely this situation. It was a canvas strap that looped through two brass plates connected by a screw. Turn the screw, and the strap would tighten sufficiently to stanch a bleeding wound. Gabe made it a point to never go into battle without one.

So why couldn't he find the blasted thing?

Then he remembered—he'd used it three hours ago on a seventeen-year-old boy from Cornwall who'd taken a bullet to his arm.

He reached for Hart's bag. "I used my tourniquet already. On Billy Portman. Which pocket do you keep yours in?"

"I used mine… too," Hart gasped.

"*Shit!*" Gabe glanced around and spotted a drummer boy just a few yards away. "Jones! Captain Lord Hartlebury has been shot. Run and find us a tourniquet, as fast as you can!"

"Yes, sir!" the boy said, sprinting back toward the British encampment.

Gabe started yanking at the knot of his neckcloth. "Steady, Hart. I—*damn this thing*—I've got you."

"N-need to ask you something." Hart gave a painful hiss as Gabe lifted his leg to slide the neckcloth underneath. "It's about A-Abbie."

"This is going to hurt," Gabe cautioned as he pulled the cravat as tight as he could.

"She's… all alone now," Hart gasped.

Hart was referring to the first calamity, the one that had arrived via letter: that Hart's parents, the Earl and Countess of Pennington, had been killed by a swift and sudden fever. Strictly speaking, this meant that Hart was no longer Viscount Hartlebury; he was now the Earl of Pennington, but that wasn't the point.

The point was that his nineteen-year-old sister, Abigail, was now all alone at the family's Hampshire estate with only servants to look after her.

Given the circumstances, the Earl of Wellington himself had granted Hart leave to return to England to bury his parents and sort out his sister's living arrangements.

Hart was planning to go.

Just as soon as they took Salamanca.

Gabe bit out a curse. He couldn't seem to get the neckcloth tight enough. Maybe his hands were too slick, or maybe the cravat was too thick, but no matter what he did, blood continued to seep from the wound. "She's not alone," Gabe said, looping the cloth around his hands for a better grip. "She's got you."

"She… she won't have me. I'm dy—"

"*Don't you dare say it*," Gabe snapped. Where the hell was Jones with the tourniquet? "I need a tourniquet!" he shouted, desperately scanning the battlefield. "You, there—Miller! Go! Get help!"

"Yes, sir!" Miller took off at a run.

"You've got to promise me," Hart said, his voice a raspy whisper.

Gabe had managed to get the cravat knotted. It wasn't tight enough, and blood still flowed from the wound, but it was the best he could do until Miller returned. He leaned over Hart, looking him in the eye, and clasped Hart's hand in his. *God*, his hand was cold. "Don't talk like that. You're not dying. Not dying, do you hear me?"

But it was more a wish than a belief, because Gabe had never seen a man so pale, and Hart was struggling to keep his eyes open. "Abbie... needs someone. To look after her. A husband. Promise me, Gabe—"

For the briefest instant, Gabe froze. Because he knew what Hart was about to ask him.

He was going to ask him to marry his sister.

Gabe wasn't on any of the lists of suitable husbands drawn up by the matchmaking mothers of the *ton*. He was a gentleman, to be sure, and one of his great-grandfathers had even been a viscount. But his father was the younger son of a younger son and had been a humble army officer, just as Gabe was today. The senior Lieutenant Davenport had left no fortune when he died, and Gabe had always known that he would have to make his own way in the world.

Marriage to a respectable young lady, and the daughter of an earl to boot, wasn't something Gabe had ever considered.

But now that he was considering it, he found the idea... strangely appealing.

Although that wasn't quite right. He wasn't thinking about marriage to any respectable young lady.

He was thinking about marriage to *Abbie*.

By the time Gabe was five years old, his parents were

both dead, and he'd spent his early years being shuttled back and forth between various uncles and cousins, none of whom were eager to have him.

When he turned seven, his great-aunt packed him off to Eton. Seven was quite a bit earlier than most boys went, but not unheard of. The viscountess made it clear to Gabe that he would not be coming home for school holidays.

But Eton wasn't all bad. After all, that was where he'd met Hart.

And then, through some miracle, the Stapleton family had more or less adopted him.

So Gabe knew Abbie. Sparkling, vivacious Abbie, who was quick with a joke, but never the kind that hurt someone's feelings. Who could make anything fun, even the most tedious parlor games like charades or blind man's bluff. Who was Gabe's favorite person to be paired with for dinner, because he never ran out of things to talk about with Abbie.

He'd always *liked* Abbie. But the last time he'd seen her, when she came to see Hart off at Dover, something had changed. She'd been sixteen years old, and Gabe hadn't seen her in a year, as they'd been busy training.

That was the day he realized she was beautiful.

But more than her pretty face and the very pleasing curves she'd developed, the thing Gabe thought of as he clasped his friend's hand in that dusty field was Abbie's letters. Hart would always read them aloud, and no matter how wretched their circumstances, how exhausted they were from the march, how many good men they'd lost, Abbie's letters made him forget it all, just for a little while. They were lively and diverting, but more than that, they gave Gabe the feeling that even in whatever shithole he found himself, there was hope. They were a reminder that there was a better world out there, and one day he would return to it.

In an instant of startling clarity, he realized that marrying

Abbie was *exactly* what he wanted. When he first joined the army, he would have scoffed at the notion of settling down and getting married. He was a young man with wild oats to sow. But whatever rakish tendencies he'd once had were now gone. Three years of war would do that to you, would make you realize what you really wanted in life.

What was truly important.

And so, in answer to Hart's *promise me, Gabe*, he squeezed his best friend's hand. "Anything."

"I'll be able to rest in peace if… if I know she's married—"

"I'll do it. I'll do it gladly."

"—to Dulson."

Gabe's body jerked, a reaction he regretted when Hart gasped in pain. "To… to Dulson?"

Hart nodded jerkily. "He'll do it. Always fancied her, Dulson has."

George Davies, Baron Dulson, had been at school with them. He hadn't been in their closest circle of friends, even though his family seat was just a couple of miles from Hart's, largely because he wasn't game for the sorts of antics they liked to get up to.

There wasn't anything *wrong* with Dulson. He was a respectable sort of chap—decent fortune, had inherited his father's barony at the age of sixteen. And he was a nice enough fellow.

But Gabe couldn't wrap his mind around the idea of someone as effervescent as Abbie marrying Dulson, who was, well…

Dull.

Below him, Hart gave a wheezing breath. "You'll make sure of it?"

"I… Yes. Of course." Gabe's voice broke, because nobody had come with a goddamn tourniquet, Hart looked as gray as a gravestone, and Gabe could no longer tell himself the lie that his favorite person on the face of this earth was not dying. "Anything, Hart."

"Then make sure she… marries Dulson."

"All right." Gabe realized that the moisture on his cheeks wasn't sweat or blood, but tears.

"Promise me."

Gabe swallowed. Nothing had changed. He'd never expected to marry a girl like Abbie. It was stupid of him to have thought of it, stupid to have imagined even for a second that Hart would want his sister to marry someone like him. He wasn't good enough for Abbie.

His own family hadn't wanted him, after all. Why should the Stapletons?

"I promise."

"One… one more thing," Hart gasped.

Gabe squeezed his best friend's hand. "Name it."

"Abbie will be… vulnerable. All alone. Looking for… comfort." Hart's eyes drifted closed, and for a horrible moment, Gabe wasn't sure if he would open them again.

But open them he did, and he looked Gabe square in the eye as he said, "Swear to me you won't touch her."

"I won't—*what?*" Gabe couldn't keep the shock and pain out of his voice.

Was *this* what Hart truly thought of him? To be sure, he was a bit of a scoundrel. But so was Hart. Gabe was under the impression that they'd had around the same number of lovers.

Gabe had to own that his reputation was worse than his friend's, but that was only because that widowed countess he'd had an affair with had been such a gossip. Lady Bollington had told half the *ton* that Gabe was surely the best lover in all of England. It had got so out of hand that the gossip rags had started reporting upon his exploits, both real and imagined.

But his reputation as some legendary rake wasn't real. It was a bunch of nonsense made up by the papers. And he certainly wasn't so low, so shameless, so *depraved* that he would take advantage of any grieving girl, much less Abbie.

Hart knew that.

Didn't he?

"Say you'll never… lay a hand on her." Hart took a gasping breath. "Swear it!"

In any other circumstance, Gabe would have been furious.

He would've asked Hart what the *hell* he was suggesting.

He would've been tempted to take a swing at his friend's jaw.

He would've demanded an apology.

In any other circumstance. But as his friend lay on the battlefield with his life bleeding out of him, Gabe did none of those things.

Instead, he brushed his thumb over his friend's cheek, wiping the spot where one of his own tears had fallen.

And he whispered, "I swear it."

That was when a pair of stretcher-bearers came rushing up.

But Gabe knew they were too late. He'd marked the moment his friend's features had fallen slack, when his eyes had gone absolutely still.

At least Hart was no longer in pain.

Gabe let the stretcher-bearers take Hart away, but he hadn't been able to summon the will to follow them.

Hart wasn't on that stretcher. Not anymore.

Instead, Gabe sat alone in that dusty field and cried until darkness fell and the sky was littered with stars.

CHAPTER 1

*L*ondon, England
July 1818
Six Years Later

YOU WOULDN'T THINK a man who'd been to war would find a roomful of women so terrifying.

But this wasn't just any roomful of women.

Gabe peered around the red velvet curtain. He was standing just offstage at the Thalia, a theater in Soho. The Thalia was smaller and less prestigious than the theaters of Covent Garden just a mile or so away, and tonight the house wasn't even close to full, with only about fifty or so in attendance.

But this particular event hadn't been intended to attract a large crowd, so much as an *exclusive* crowd.

An entirely feminine crowd.

A crowd that could keep a secret.

Most of those assembled had come in quasi-masquerade dress, with masks and dominoes concealing their features.

Not that this prevented him from recognizing a few familiar faces. The woman with the flame-red hair had to be Mrs. Seymour, an attractive widow of perhaps thirty-five years, and standing next to her was Veronique Lacroix, a successful actress with whom Gabe had conducted an affair many years ago. They had ended their liaison on good terms, and Gabe counted Veronique as a friend. Never one to shy away from a scandal, she hadn't even bothered to wear a mask.

He also recognized the woman in the green dress as Lady Liddell, who was young, pretty, and spoiled. She had been married for less than a year to a man twenty years her senior. Lord Liddell doted on his feisty young bride, even if he had absolutely no idea what to do with her, and Gabe was certain he would not approve of her presence here tonight.

Oh, dear—and there in the back row was Lady Walsington, who was old enough to be his grandmother.

Although honestly, he would prefer Lady Walsington to Lady Liddell. Gabe might be a scoundrel, but he did have some standards, and one of those involved not sleeping with a married woman unless she had that sort of arrangement with her husband.

But it looked like he might be about to kiss those standards goodbye because the reason they were all assembled tonight was for London's most notorious bachelor auction. The winner of each lot was purchasing one night with their chosen lover.

And, given his current level of desperation, Gabe had no choice but to enter.

He stepped back, letting the curtain drop. Not that anyone had been looking at him. Every pair of eyes in the room was fixed upon the shirtless man at center stage.

The Thalia's proprietress, Madame Heron, spoke in a voice that carried in the mostly empty theater. "As I'm sure you know, Tom Talbot is the reigning heavyweight champion. Believe me, ladies, you won't find another specimen like this! Tommy, love, show us the goods, won't you?"

Talbot brought his fists up by his head, flexing his arms. This elicited a chorus of oohs and aahs from the crowd. Grinning, Talbot struck a series of poses, each garnering more cheers than the last, until he turned around, showing off back muscles Gabe hadn't known existed in a grand finale that all but incited a riot.

Madame Heron stepped forward and trailed a hand along Talbot's biceps. "As you can see, this is a once-in-a-lifetime opportunity. May I have a starting bid of twenty pounds?"

A dozen hands shot into the air. Gabe observed the bidding from the wings. Most of those assembled bowed out around the fifty-pound mark, but a pair emerged who seemed determined to claim the prize. One wore a hood instead of a mask, probably because of the spectacles Gabe could just make out glinting from beneath her cowl. She was short and plump and had a cringing sort of posture suggesting she dearly wished she could sink beneath the carpet. Her plain, frumpy dress buttoned all the way up to her chin and practically screamed, *don't look at me.*

Her only real problem was that she didn't know how to flatter those curves. Put her in a less dowdy frock and she would be delectable.

Her competition for the boxing champion was the young Lady Liddell.

"Seventy-two pounds!" Miss Spectacles called in a voice that shook.

Lady Liddell shot her rival a smirk. "Seventy-three pounds."

"Seventy-four pounds."

"Oh, are we going to do this all night? One hundred pounds," Lady Liddell called.

The room fell silent. This was the highest bid that had been placed thus far, and Lady Liddell's smile was triumphant.

Madame Heron had just raised her arm to declare Lady Liddell the winner when Miss Spectacles cried out in a shrill voice, "Two hundred and fifty pounds!"

The room fell silent. Lady Liddell's smirk melted into a scowl. Seeing that the bidding was over, Madame Heron pointed to Miss Spectacles, declaring, "We have a winner!"

Tom Talbot grinned and jumped right off the stage. He waded through the crowd of women, several of whom reached out to squeeze his arm or stroke his chest as he passed, until he reached his purchaser. He was a good foot taller than Miss Spectacles. Much to her apparent shock, he swept her up in his arms and pressed her high against his chest. "Gonna make it worth every penny, love," he said loudly enough for the entire room to hear. He proceeded to carry her down the aisle of the theater and right out the door while those behind him whistled and cheered.

As the crowd quieted, Gabe heard Lady Liddell declare for the benefit of those around her, "I could've bought him if I wanted to. I'm just making sure I have enough blunt to secure the man I *truly* desire."

Gabe groaned. Given that he was the only one left, that didn't bode well for him being able to stick to his personal code.

Madame Heron waited for the crowd to quiet. "And now, for our final bachelor of the evening!"

Gabe swallowed. To have to go out there after the reigning heavyweight champion—talk about a hard act to follow. But there was no bowing out now.

Desperate times called for desperate measures. And there wasn't a man in England more desperate than Gabriel Davenport.

Madame Heron was really working up the crowd. "He's the one you've aaaaaall been waiting for! A man who needs no introduction, such is his reputation for giving his lovers *unimaginable* pleasure!"

"*Oui*," Veronique called out from the back row of the theater. "I can attest, it is true."

Over the titters that filled the room, Madame Heron called, "And it is therefore my pleasure—although the pleasure will soon belong to one of you—to present England's most talented lover, Gabriel Davenport!"

Well, there was nothing for it. Gabe pasted a devil-may-care smile on his face and strode out onto the stage, waving to the crowd.

As Madame Heron had instructed, he was dressed in nothing but a fine linen shirt which he wore gaping open to his sternum, top boots, and a pair of skintight midnight blue pantaloons. The ladies burst into cheers.

Madame Heron gave them a moment to settle down. "Now, tonight is more significant than you realize. I'm sure most of you have heard the news that London's favorite scoundrel is now a viscount."

Polite applause filled the theater as if Gabe had done something to earn this honor. In truth, his great-uncle, the fourth Viscount Fairbourne, had been sailing for Jamaica with both of his sons and their families, hoping to escape his creditors and restore the family fortunes, when the ship was lost in a storm. In an instant, the next seven men in line to inherit the viscountcy were gone, and Gabe found himself in a situation he'd never imagined would come to pass.

But along with his great-uncle's title, Gabe had inherited the man's debts, which were right around fifty thousand pounds. By the time he received word of his uncle's passing and managed to get back from Malta, where he'd been stationed, the sharks were closing in. Thanks to his new status as a peer, Gabe couldn't be thrown in debtor's prison, but his creditors could ransack the family homes and seize anything that wasn't nailed down.

Including, as his great aunt Matilda tearfully told him, her wedding ring.

Great-aunt Matilda happened to be the one who'd packed Gabe off to Eton at the age of seven. But he wasn't so hard-hearted that he would deny a seventy-seven-year-old woman who had just lost her husband, both of her children, and all of her grandchildren one memento to cling to.

What Gabe needed was a spectacularly rich heiress who was willing to marry him for his title. Gabe was confident he could find someone. There were plenty of coal barons looking to marry their daughter to a peer.

He just needed more than one bloody week to do it.

He'd managed to strike a deal with the creditors. If Gabe could come up with five hundred pounds as a show of good faith, they would delay the seizure of the estate's effects for one month. Great-aunt Matilda could keep her wedding ring, and Gabe would have just enough breathing room to locate and marry a suitable heiress.

All he had to do, he mused, gazing out over the crowd of women in the theater below, was convince someone in this room that a night in his bed was worth five hundred pounds.

Madame Heron continued her speech. "Now, I'm sure that most of us are aware that the new Lord Fairbourne here is on the hunt for a wealthy bride." She paused, a gleam in her eye. "But I know something that I believe will come as a shock. This very evening, Lord Fairbourne told me that once he marries, he intends to be faithful to his wife!"

Wails of protest filled the gallery below. Madame Heron held her hands up for silence. "That's right, the person with the highest bid tonight might very well be the last lover Lord Fairbourne ever takes. The last woman, save for his new bride, to ever experience the exquisite pleasure that only he can give."

Gabe affected a sheepish smile and an apologetic shrug. But this had been an easy decision. The world thought he was a complete and total scoundrel.

Hell, he thought, recalling Hart lying in that field, warning Gabe off his sister. Even his best friend thought he was irredeemable.

But that wasn't how Gabe saw himself, nor was it who he wanted to be. All of his past antics had taken place before he turned twenty-three. They were youthful follies, nothing more. He'd hardly been in the country for the last nine years, for Christ's sake, and opportunities to have a torrid affair had been thin on the ground during his dusty deployments. But his reputation as this legendary rakehell somehow refused to die.

He knew he needed to choose a rich bride, but Gabe also hoped he might find someone he could... not love. There was only one woman he thought he could truly love, and in a cruel twist of fate, she happened to be the one woman he could never have. But he wanted to give his marriage a chance, and that meant he wasn't going to be hopping in and out of every bed in Mayfair.

Madame Heron continued, "So keep that in mind as you're considering how much you want to bid." She turned to Gabe. "Lord Fairbourne, if you would be so kind as to show these esteemed ladies what they're bidding on?"

Gabe grinned, trying to look as if he was enjoying himself, and peeled his shirt up over his head. As one, the crowd of women made an appreciative *ooh*.

Gabe might not be the heavyweight champion of England, but the nine years he'd spent in the army had been good for something. He was six foot two with broad shoulders and strong arms from countless hours spent fencing, shooting, hauling water, and building a camp then tearing it down three days later. His hips were slim from endless days spent riding and marching, and his body was toned and well-muscled, with nary an ounce of fat on it. His torso was a golden tan just a shade lighter than his blond hair from all those afternoons they'd spent sea-bathing on Malta.

He wasn't about to strike a prizefighter's pose the way Tom Talbot had done; there were some acts a man simply could not follow. But he gave his best rakish grin and made eye contact with as many of the assembled ladies as he could, even running a hand slowly through his hair.

Madame Heron clapped her hands. "May I have an opening bid of fifty pounds?"

Half of those present raised their hands, which was a good sign. But not enough to allow Gabe to relax. He needed the bidding to get up over five hundred pounds if he was going to delay his creditors. And considering that only one other man had broken the hundred-pound mark, that was a hell of a tall order.

From the gallery, Veronique gave him a nod. She knew his situation and was the one who had suggested the auction in the first place. She'd also called in a favor with Madame Heron, and unlike the other bachelors, who had to pay a cut of their sales price to the house, Gabe would be keeping his full proceeds.

He knew he could count on Veronique to run the bidding up a bit, and she entered the fray with a bid of seventy-five pounds. At that point, a dozen women were bidding for a night of Gabe's company.

When the bidding reached one hundred and fifty pounds, it was down to four.

When it crossed the two-hundred-pound mark, there were only two: Veronique and Lady Liddell.

Gabe knew he had to maintain his devil-may-care front,

but he shot Veronique a speaking look, silently begging her to stay in there. More important than age or attractiveness, he wanted to be purchased by someone who was unencumbered. Sleeping with Lady Liddell, whose husband would be heartbroken by the betrayal, was the opposite of who he was trying to be.

Veronique kept bidding, but as Gabe's price rose, her face became increasingly drawn. Finally, when the bidding passed three hundred fifty pounds, she shot Gabe an apologetic look and shook her head.

Shit. Not only was he going to have to sleep with Lady Liddell, he'd fallen a hundred and fifty pounds shy of the sum he needed to delay his creditors. He was going to have to betray his values, and it wouldn't even save Great-aunt Matilda's wedding ring.

Gabe forced a smile to his lips and turned to face Lady Liddell.

That was when he saw her.

She'd been lingering in the shadows at the back of the room. Unlike most of the ladies, who had dressed for a masquerade, her black silk gown looked like it had been designed for mourning, especially as she had paired it with a black lace veil that completely obscured her face.

For some reason, as this mystery woman began making her way down the theater's aisle, Gabe felt the hairs on the back of his neck prickle and stand on end.

He didn't know who she was, but he felt a sudden, overwhelming certainty that she was *someone*.

The crowd fell silent as she walked to the front of the room. Gabe could see nothing of her face behind that veil, but he could tell she was looking him straight in the eye.

Once she had reached the front of the gallery, she stopped, then said in a voice that was both certain and tremulous, "One thousand pounds."

The room exploded with excitement. Lady Liddell's face looked as dark as the Thames at midnight. Veronique's relief was almost palpable.

Madame Heron nodded regally. "One thousand pounds. Everyone, a round of applause for our winner!"

Gabe dropped his shirt back over his head as he crossed the stage and hopped down before his purchaser. He could still see nothing of her face in the candlelight. He took her hand, clad in an elbow-length black kidskin glove, and bowed over it. "My lady," he said, as his best guess was that a woman with such an elegant bearing would be titled. He gestured up the aisle. "Shall we?"

She nodded crisply and took his arm. "We shall."

And with that, Gabriel led his black-silk-clad savior out into the night.

CHAPTER 2

The carriage Madame Heron had waiting for them was perfect: unmarked black lacquer on the outside, plush gray velvet on the inside.

Gabe handed the woman in black up into the carriage, then paused as he followed, unsure if he should sit next to her or take the facing seat. Normally he would not presume. But considering the circumstances…

Seeing her ramrod-straight drawing room posture, he opted for the facing seat.

After a few seconds of silence, Gabe said, "Thank you."

The veil-clad head turned to regard him. "For what?"

"For purchasing me. Instead of Lady Liddell. I—" He paused, considering his words. "I've never slept with a married woman before, unless she had that sort of arrangement with her husband. I wasn't keen to start."

"Of course not. You would never do that," she murmured.

"What was that?" he asked, startled. It sounded almost as if she knew him.

Yet he had no idea who she might be.

She waved a black-gloved hand. "Never mind."

He blanched as it occurred to him that his purchaser might be in much the same situation as Lady Liddell. "For all I know, you might be married, too," he said cautiously.

"I'm not. I'm a widow."

The tension that had crept into his shoulders abruptly eased. "That's a relief." He studied her in the moonlight filtering through the carriage windows. He still couldn't make out anything of her face, but she was of medium height and had a splendid figure with lush breasts and a deliciously curved bottom. It would be no chore to bed this woman. "You can take that off if you like," he said, gesturing to his own face. "I'll find out who you are soon enough. Unless"—he grinned, and it felt natural, the first smile he hadn't had to feign since the start of this bizarre evening—"that's something you like. To wear your veil, and nothing else."

Her voice was prim. "I do not wish to be seen on the way to our room. I will remove it once we're safely inside."

He inclined his head. "As you prefer."

The carriage slowed as they approached their destination: Pulteney House, London's finest hotel, located just north of Green Park. Instead of pulling up to the main entrance, the carriage went around to the back, and they were ushered in via the servants' entrance. A footman led them directly to a suite on the top floor.

Gabe had never had occasion to enter the Pulteney before, but the room was as lush as he'd expected. Axminster carpets adorned a hardwood floor so glossy it gleamed in the candlelight. Curtains of Prussian blue velvet, corded in gold, had been drawn over windows that ran almost the full height of the wall. Not that there was much to see at this time of night, but during the day, the view of Green Park must be spectacular. Scenes from Greek myths adorned frescos that lined the walls. And the plush satin counterpane upon the bed was a bright, immaculate white.

The room had been prepared for them. The satchel Gabe had given Madame Heron was waiting in the dressing area, and his change of clothes was neatly hung, ready for the next morning.

Gabe also noticed a few items set upon the bedside table: two bottles containing different types of oil, a neat stack of towels, and a tall glass of water with a number of translucent strips floating around inside: sheepskin condoms, pre-soaked and ready for use.

Gabe strode over to the sideboard and poured himself a brandy. "Would you like something?" he asked his companion. Glancing over his shoulder, he saw that she had begun to unpin her veil. He kept one eye on her, eager to see who his companion for the evening might be. "There's champagne, sherry, and hot water if you'd prefer tea."

The veil had become snagged on something—most probably a hairpin—and she was carefully working to untangle it. "Is there any Madeira?"

"There is," Gabe confirmed, turning to pour it. He couldn't help but smile as he did so. "You've made me think of my best friend's little sister. She always preferred Madeira."

He turned with their drinks in hand. She'd managed to work the veil free, and Gabe watched as she pulled it up and over her head. Her back was to him, but the first thing he noticed was her hair, piled atop her head, neither brown nor blonde, but a lovely shade of caramel.

She turned her head, glancing at him over her shoulder. The glasses suddenly slipped in his hands as he met a pair of familiar eyes—huge and aquamarine blue, the same color as the sea off the coast of Malta. He managed not to drop their drinks entirely, but most of the glasses' contents went sloshing onto his boots.

"And she still does," Abigail said, smiling as she tossed her veil onto a chair.

CHAPTER 3

Abbie regarded Gabe in the candlelight.

She'd been wondering how he would react once he learned that she was the winner of the auction. While she had prepared herself for a range of possible responses, she'd allowed herself to hope his reaction would be positive, despite what had happened last time.

Last time being the four-day interval in which she had buried her brother, married a man she did not love, and moved out of the only home she had ever known, all while the only friend she had left in the world remained hell-bent on avoiding her.

When Gabe returned home with Hart's body, Abbie had been a wreck. Her parents had died the previous month, and Gabe's letter informing her of her brother's death on the battlefield had beaten him to Hampshire by a mere two days. On the day Gabe arrived, she was still reeling from the news that instead of reuniting with her brother, she was going to bury him.

She hadn't known what to expect from their meeting. Frankly, she hadn't been thinking clearly enough to even form expectations. But she knew that Gabe was the only person on the face of this earth who had loved Hart as much as she had, and who felt his loss, as well as the loss of her parents, as deeply. She had assumed they would comfort one another.

When Gabe got out of the carriage, dusty from the road and deeply tan from years spent in the field, Abbie burst into tears. She came flying down the steps of Pennington House and threw her arms around his neck.

Or at least, she tried to. Instead of catching her in a hug and letting her cry on his shoulder, Gabe recoiled, all but scrambling back into the carriage.

Abbie quickly recalled that most men had a horror of weeping women. She'd known that, but in her defense, she had a host of other troubles on her mind.

Still, she understood Gabe's reaction. But she didn't appreciate the way he had recoiled after giving her his handkerchief. She hadn't meant to brush his fingers, but her hands were trembling. The way he'd jerked back at the contact, you'd have thought she was stricken with some sort of plague.

The next four days were not an improvement. Instead of commiserating with Abbie, Gabe went straight to her uncle Edmund, the new earl. Uncle Edmund had five daughters of his own who now needed to be outfitted and dowered in a manner befitting the daughters of a peer. He immediately warmed to the idea of marrying Abbie off to the man chosen by her own brother. Lord Dulson, whose home was just two miles away, was promptly summoned. It came as little surprise to Abbie that Dulson, who had proposed on three previous occasions, was ready and willing to comply with her brother's dying wish. When he offered to take Abbie without a dowry, her fate had been sealed.

Abbie tried to protest. As she had told Lord Dulson whilst

declining his three previous proposals, she did not love him and felt certain that she never would. Besides, it was unbecoming for her to marry anyone so quickly upon the deaths of her parents and brother. Her uncle would hear none of it, so she attempted to appeal to Gabe. But Gabe spent the scant days he was there avoiding her, quitting any room she entered and excusing himself the second she attempted to engage him in conversation.

Meanwhile, her aunt and uncle spent their days lecturing Abbie, telling her what a bad sister she was for refusing her brother's dying wish, that there would not be enough money to dower both her and her cousins, and what an unfeeling, selfish girl she was not to think of them.

In the end, marriage to a man she knew she would never love had seemed a better choice than life inside a house where she was unwanted, scorned, and constantly hounded. Seeing no alternative, two days after burying her brother, Abbie married Lord Dulson.

Gabe left as soon as the parish registry was signed, not even staying for the wedding breakfast.

None of that suggested that their next meeting would be on good terms.

But then, the strangest thing happened.

Six months later, feeling almost as lonely and forlorn as she had on her wedding day, Abbie found herself writing a letter to Gabe. It wasn't a normal sort of letter. No, this was a mawkish, pour-your-heart-out sort of letter, full of all of the messy emotions he apparently couldn't stand.

She hadn't meant to post it. She'd thought it might be cathartic to write everything down and then throw those feelings into the fire. But she left it out on her desk, meaning to read it over one last time before destroying it, and a housemaid picked it up and placed it in the stack of outgoing correspondence. Her husband franked everything in the pile without looking to see what it was, and out into the world it had gone.

Abbie was horrified when she learned the letter had been posted. She spent the next few months in agony, wondering what Gabe must think of her and dreading his response, if she received one at all.

But when Gabe's letter came… it was *wonderful*. He didn't seem to mind her jumbled emotions; in fact, he confessed to feeling much the same way. Whereas everyone else kept telling her to bear up, to move on, Gabe told her that her grief was natural, that the fact that she loved her parents and brother so deeply was a mark of what a good person she was. He even apologized for his stilted behavior during his brief time in Hampshire, saying he knew he knew he had handled it in the worst manner imaginable.

Abbie wrote back at once. It was such a relief to finally have someone who understood. And so, she and Gabe struck up a correspondence, a correspondence that became Abbie's lifeline. To be sure, Gabe's letters weren't what you would call *cheerful*. He was, after all, fighting in a war, as well as mourning the loss of his closest friend. But then, neither were hers. And more importantly, his letters were the one place she could express her honest feelings, where she could be sad or angry, where she didn't have to put on a jolly face and pretend that everything was splendid when it wasn't. Gabe wrote back confessing how lonely he felt without Hart, and how hard it was to maintain the stoic front expected of an army officer. And Abbie had the comfort of knowing that even if he was hundreds of miles away, at least someone out there understood.

After five years of exchanging such letters, Abbie felt closer to Gabe than she'd ever felt to anyone. And so she had allowed herself to entertain the hope that he *might* be happy to see her.

Of course, she'd known his reaction might not be positive. That he might still think of her as a child rather than a woman and balk at the prospect of making love to her. Or he might feel embarrassed that she'd seen him at such a low moment when he was forced to sell himself to the highest bidder.

Yet even though she had prepared herself for a negative reaction, the abject horror on his face…

It certainly wasn't *flattering*.

She pasted on a smile. "Good evening, Gabe. So lovely to see you again." She waited a beat for a reply, but he seemed to be at a complete loss. She peeled off her gloves. "May I have my drink? I suddenly feel as though I could use one."

She reached for her glass, but when she was an inch from taking it, he jerked backward, bumping into the sideboard and spilling the remaining Madeira on his boots.

She sighed. So this was the way of it. The Gabe she'd come to know so well, the one who'd written her those wonderful letters, was gone. They were right back to where they'd been at Hart's funeral.

"I'll just pour another, shall I?" she said, reaching for her glass. Gabe set it down on the sideboard and scooted away with a rather uncomplimentary alacrity.

She was removing the stopper from the decanter when he blurted, "What are you doing here?"

"Considering you were present during the key moments of the evening, one would assume you might know." She took a fortifying sip from her glass, then turned to face him. "I purchased you." He continued staring at her, his face completely blank, so she added, "In the bachelor auction."

He blinked and shook his head. "Yes. But why would *you* bid on *me*?"

He was going to make her spell it out.

Lovely.

"My reasons were twofold. I must confess, the reason I opened with a bid of one thousand pounds, rather than trying to obtain you for the lowest possible price, is because your financial difficulties have become common knowledge." She bit her lip. "I consider you to be my friend, Gabe. One of my dearest friends. I hope you won't take it the wrong way when I say that I wanted to help you."

He sagged against the sideboard, relief washing over his face. "You're the best, Abbie. I can't say how much I appreciate it." He snagged the brandy, refilling his own glass. "I'll pay you back. I swear I will. Just as soon as I've found some heiress who'll have me." He turned to face her, grinning as he raised his glass. He paused just shy of taking a sip and said, "It's such a relief to know you were just helping an old friend. That you don't mean to collect on your purchase."

"Oh, I mean to collect on it," she said.

He promptly choked on his brandy and came up coughing.

Based on his previous displays of horror at the most incidental contact, she decided it best not to thump him on the back.

Once he recovered, he regarded her, wild-eyed. "What do you mean, you intend to collect on it? You said—"

"I said that my reasons for purchasing you were twofold. One was a desire to help you during a rough patch. As for the other…" She could feel heat rising in her cheeks, but she forced herself to continue. "I daresay it is the same reason as every other woman in that room."

He looked so aghast, you'd have thought she'd just pulled out a gun and shot his dog. "You can't mean… *You* want to…" He pointed to her, and then to himself. "With *me*?"

Oh, good gracious—did it really come as such a shock? He was widely hailed as the most handsome man, and the most skillful lover, in all of England! Every other woman wanted to make love with him.

Why should she be any different?

Although in truth, it was more than that. Abbie had always had an infatuation with Gabe, which was unsurprising. What girl didn't have a *tendre* for her brother's best friend, especially when he looked like a golden Greek god?

But that had just been a schoolgirl's fancy.

It was not until they had begun exchanging letters that Abbie's feelings for Gabe had deepened. And, of course, she hadn't seen him in six years. She might find him very different than the man she thought she knew through his letters.

But she really thought there was a chance that he was the love of her life. And if losing her parents and brother in the space of one month had taught her anything, it was that life was as precious as it was fleeting. Never again would she miss a chance to chase after her dreams.

And she knew full well that her dream of Gabe was doomed. All of London was talking about how he needed an heiress with more than fifty thousand pounds to clear the old viscount's debts. Abbie's husband had left her a dower house and a little nest egg, but nowhere near that amount.

And, considering recent events, there was an alarmingly high chance she was going to lose what meager funds she had.

It was indisputable. He couldn't marry her. She couldn't have forever.

But she could have tonight.

So, refusing to feel ashamed, Abbie drew herself up and gave her most regal nod. "I do."

"But… but…" He was glancing wildly about the room,

looking anywhere but at her. "Why would you want to do that?"

"Let's see, where to begin?" She downed the rest of her drink for courage, then set the glass on the sideboard. "I believe you are aware that I was married to Lord Dulson."

"Of course. What of it?"

Through gritted teeth, she asked, "Is that not sufficient explanation?"

He pushed off from the sideboard and began pacing the room. "I'm sure marriage to Dulson was, er, satisfactory."

She crossed her arms. "I just spent a thousand pounds to spend one night with you. Is that the mark of someone whose marriage bed was *satisfactory*?"

She could tell by his rueful expression that he understood completely, but he chose to soldier on. "You're probably imagining there's more to it than there is. I'm sure my, er, *performance*, is not materially different from Dulson's."

"I'm not so sure." Abbie paused, searching for the right words. "Am I correct in my understanding that it is possible for the woman to enjoy it?"

Gabe bit off a string of curses, the least offensive of which were *bloody* and *hell*. He crossed the room in three strides and poured himself another brandy. Seeing her raised eyebrow, he bit out, "I'm sorry. I've been in the army for nine years. I've forgotten how to comport myself in the presence of a lady."

She stepped forward, raising her hands to stroke his chest. "I'll bet you haven't forgotten *everything* about being with a—confound it, Gabe!" she cried when he again went scrambling backward.

She stalked across the room after him. He kept retreating until he was all the way in the corner.

"Why," she asked, her voice rich with annoyance, "do you keep doing that?"

CHAPTER 4

*A*bbie studied Gabe. There was a wild-eyed quality to his expression, like an animal caught in a snare.

Which she supposed was apt. She had him cornered.

And she wasn't about to let him go. Not until he'd explained what was going on.

"D-doing what?" he sputtered.

Oh, that was rich—pretending his behavior was perfectly normal! Abbie's hands curled into fists. "Recoiling from me as if I have some sort of contagious rash!"

"I, uh…"

She couldn't shout because goodness knows how many people would hear through the thin walls of the hotel, so she had to settle for hissing. "You entered yourself in a *bachelor auction*! You knew you would have to make love to the winner, whoever she was. That was what *you* agreed to." To her mortification, her voice was shaking, and her vision was blurred by tears. "Am I really so hideous that you can't bear the thought of going through with it?"

"No!" He stepped forward, hands held out placatingly.

"You're not hideous at all. You're the opposite of hideous. Just look at you, Abbie—you're gorgeous!"

"Then why are you so openly horrified at the prospect of making love with me?"

"I wouldn't say I'm horrified, precisely."

She glared at him. "Is this the legendary charm of the greatest lover in England?"

A blush crept over his cheeks, discernible despite his golden tan. "You're not supposed to know about that."

"I wasn't supposed to know about your reputation when I was fourteen and you were twenty, but I did, because absolutely everybody was talking about it. But allow me to point out that I am no longer fourteen." She made a sweeping gesture from her shoulders to her feet. "I am a woman of twenty-five, married and widowed, and there is no reason I might not read the scandal sheets like everyone else." She studied him. The panic in his eyes was not feigned. "Is that the problem, Gabe? That you still think of me as a little girl instead of a woman?"

He laughed blackly. "Believe me, that's not it."

As he was now standing in profile to her, Abbie had an unimpeded view of his pantaloons, so tight they left absolutely nothing to the imagination.

She sucked in a breath as she studied the heavy bulge straining against his falls. Indeed, it appeared that a lack of physical attraction was not the problem.

"Well, what is it, then? Do you think it unseemly for me to want to make love to a man who can actually make it good for me?" She felt tears pricking at the back of her eyes. "Because I do want that. My husband, God rest his soul, was not a bad man, but he didn't know a single thing about pleasing a woman. And my next husband looks just as unpromising."

He rounded on her. "What do you mean, your next husband? Are you betrothed to another?"

"I am not. But I've received an offer of marriage, and I might be forced to accept it."

He crossed his arms. "Explain."

She shook her head. "I'd rather not."

Worry stole into Gabe's eyes. "Are you destitute?"

"No." Which was true, strictly speaking.

Although if Nigel Davies, the cousin who had inherited the barony from her deceased husband, had his way, she soon would be.

But she didn't want to get into all of that with Gabe, at least not right now. He would probably leap at any chance to change the topic of conversation, whereas she was determined not to let it veer off course. So she added, "Although he was not obliged to do so, George left me a small inheritance."

That much, at least, was true. George had been more than generous. Although Abbie had brought nothing to the marriage, when her husband's will was read, she found that he had left her the dower house, a charmingly situated building with a dozen rooms on the edge of the Dulson estate, and enough money to live out her life in a modest-but-respectable sort of way.

But then, at loose ends during her year of mourning, Abbie had undertaken to sort through the centuries of odds and ends left behind by the Dowager Ladies Dulson who had occupied the little stone house before her. And she had found more than rusted hairpins and chipped teacups.

She had found a secret.

A dark, terrible secret, one Nigel would stop at nothing to bury.

And so Abbie found herself caught in the crossfire, torn between decency and survival.

She cleared her throat. "Although I am not destitute, there is a possibility that I will have to marry a man I would rather not have."

"I won't allow it," Gabe said hotly. "I won't let anyone force you to marry against your will."

Abbie's voice was brittle as she replied, "Would that you had expressed such a sentiment six years ago."

Misery flooded his eyes, and she felt a pang of guilt. They had hashed all of this out in their letters, after all. Abbie had enough pages of Gabe's apologies for pressing her to marry George to fill… perhaps not a *proper* book.

But a penny dreadful? Most probably.

"You're right," Gabe said in a rush. "You're absolutely right, and I'm sorry I—"

"Wait, Gabe. Stop. I shouldn't have said that. I—"

"No, I'm glad you said it. An apology by letter can never contain the proper depth of feeling." His green eyes were earnest. "I would gladly kneel at your feet. There's nothing I wouldn't do to earn your forgiveness."

"I know that." She reached for his hand. "I know you are sincerely sorry. It was churlish of me to say such a thing."

He shook his head. "You are more generous than I—gah!"

Gabe recoiled at the brush of Abbie's fingers against the back of his hand, curling halfway into a ball and pressing himself against the wall.

Abbie sighed. So this was how it was to be.

She cleared her throat. "It happens that I do not want to discuss my marital prospects. Nor do I wish to hear another apology. You may rest assured that I have every confidence in your sincerity and that I have forgiven you. What I wish to discuss is *this*," she said, gesturing to the three feet of space that separated them.

"This?" Gabe asked, eyes slightly wild as if he were searching for a route of escape. "This is nothing."

She took a step forward, and he recoiled into the wall. She repressed the urge to stomp her foot. "This is hardly nothing if we are to make love!"

He wouldn't meet her eye. "Why do you want to do that with me, anyway?"

This did not seem like a promising moment to inform Gabe that she was fairly certain he was the love of her life. So instead, Abbie said, "We have already established that my marriage bed was unsatisfactory. And, to make matters worse, I may soon be wed to a man who isn't one whit better." She heard her voice break at the thought of marrying Nigel, who shared all of her former husband's failings but lacked George's great compensatory quality: kindness.

Lifting her chin, she soldiered on. "But before I do, I want to do something for myself. I want to experience pleasure, the kind that can exist between a man and a woman. And I refuse to feel ashamed for wanting that."

Gabe's eyes were tender as he stepped forward. "God, Abbie, I would never judge you for that." He raised a hand to brush an errant lock of hair back from her forehead. "You deserve a competent lover not just for one night, but every—gah!" He jerked back, staring at his hand in horror. "God damn it! I mustn't do that!"

"Mustn't do what? Touch me?" She laughed incredulously. "I should like to know how we're going to make love without touching one another!"

He slashed a hand in front of him. "We're not going to make love."

"*You* were the one who *just said* I deserved a competent lover!"

"You do. But it will have to be someone else."

She crossed her arms. "Then you intend to return my thousand pounds?"

He groaned and rubbed the heel of his hand against an

eye. "Is there any way you'd let me hang onto it? Just as a loan?" He looked at her then, and his green eyes were beseeching. "My uncle's creditors are on the cusp of seizing the contents of the house, and in particular, my Great-aunt Matilda's wedding ring. If I can come up with five hundred pounds, they've agreed to delay a month."

Her jaw all but fell to the floor. "Do you mean to tell me that the reason you entered that bachelor auction was so your Great-aunt Matilda could keep her wedding ring?"

"Yes."

"The same Great-aunt Matilda who shipped you off to Eton when you were seven years old and wouldn't even let you come home for Christmas?"

"The very one."

She gaped at him. That he would go to such lengths to help the woman who had cast him out was incomprehensible. "Why, Gabe? Why would you put yourself in such a position for someone who treated you so callously?"

He fell silent. "I know you probably think I'm an irredeemable cad. Goodness knows everyone else does. But that's not how I see myself. And even if she doesn't much deserve my help, I don't want to be the type of person who laughs at the troubles of a seventy-seven-year-old woman who's just lost everyone she loves."

Abbie noted Gabe's clenched fist, his drawn brow, and the way he spat out the word *cad*. She had clearly found a sore spot. "No, Gabe. I've never thought you were a cad, and I'm sorry if I gave that impression. I only meant that not one person in a hundred would bother to help your great-aunt after what she did. What you're doing is exceptional."

Gabe shrugged and looked away. Abbie regarded him in the candlelight. The fact that he was helping his great-aunt, who could not have deserved it less, just went to show that

Gabe was the wonderful, caring man she'd come to know through his letters, not the cold stranger who'd pushed her into a marriage she didn't want four years ago. She'd been right about him all along.

And she was determined to have him.

At least for tonight. If that was all she could ever have of Gabe, at least she would have this one night to look back on when she was old and gray and alone.

And to be sure, he was still eyeing her as if she were a rabid dog.

But if the large bulge pressing against the falls of his trousers was any indication, he wasn't *entirely* indifferent to her.

Slowly, cautiously, she took a step forward. He took a corresponding step back. She took another step forward, causing him to retreat. They did it again, and again.

"Abbie," he grumbled.

"Why are we doing this?" she asked brightly.

He bumped into a chair along the wall and was forced to stop. "D-doing what?"

"This dance. The Don't-Touch-Abbie dance."

He swallowed thickly, which drew her eyes down to his throat and the open vee of white linen framing his golden chest. "I-I don't know what you're talking about."

She raised a hand and feigned poking him in the shoulder. He dodged to the side, so she repeated the motion on the opposite shoulder. This time he reversed course so sharply he tripped over the chair and had to grab its back for purchase.

He glared at her. "Damn it, Abbie."

"Now that we've established that you're avoiding me—"

"We've established—ugh"—he ducked to the side again, narrowly avoiding her teasing finger and winding up all the way in the corner—"nothing."

"—you may as well tell me why."

He crossed his arms. "I confess nothing."

"Fine!" She waved a hand. "Stand there as long as you like. You're not going anywhere until you tell me what's going on."

He leaned forward, his eyes full of challenge. "Maybe I'll just leave."

Slowly, sensuously, she leaned forward, too. He recoiled, which she'd been expecting, but she kept going, purposefully placing her hands on the wall on either side of his broad shoulders, trapping him in the corner. She dropped her gaze to his lips. "Go right ahead."

Of course, there was no escaping without touching her, and Abbie marked the moment he realized his predicament. "Please just let me go." The consternation on his face was real, and it tore at her heart to see it.

"I will gladly let you go if that's what you really want. I hope you know, Gabe, that I would never force you to make love to me if you do not want to, in spite of the fact that you put yourself up for sale to the highest bidder tonight."

"Thank you," he murmured, his gaze softening.

"But," she added, casting a significant glance down toward the bulge in the front of his pantaloons, "I am no longer an ignorant virgin. We both know that you're not entirely indifferent to me."

He blanched, glancing down and then scanning their surroundings, presumably looking for a pillow or some such to hold in front of his groin. Finding nothing of use, he had to settle for untucking his shirt. "Never mind that."

"Oh, I mind it. I mind it very much. And although I am willing to let you go, I will only do so after you've explained the reasoning behind your bizarre behavior."

"You're imagining things—gah!" He dodged as best he could within the confines of her arms as she slowly raised her lips toward the slope of his jaw. But mixed in with the panic, she could see desire, raw and hot, flood his eyes.

"You're right," she murmured, her lips an inch away from the spot where his pulse throbbed in his neck. "You don't want to make love to me, not even a little bit. And all of this is completely normal."

His eyes took on a pleading look. "Please don't make me tell you."

"*Tell me.*"

"But I-I—" She blew softly on his neck, and his whole body shuddered. "I promised your brother."

Her brother? That didn't make any sense. Hart couldn't have anything to do with this.

He'd been dead for six years.

The word *promise* scratched at the back of her brain. He'd promised Hart he would see her married to George. That was the only promise Gabe had made.

Or so she had thought.

Slowly, she raised her gaze to meet his. "What did you promise my brother?"

Gabe's eyes were sad. The only time she'd seen him look so defeated was when they lowered Hart's body into the ground four years ago. When he spoke, his voice was the merest whisper. "I promised him that I would never touch you."

CHAPTER 5

*T*hat *idiot.*

Abbie loved her brother and missed him every day.

But what an absolutely cod-headed thing to have done.

Gabe was now staring at the floor, dejected. She wanted to sweep her hand along his jaw and raise his eyes to hers, but of course, he was terrified of her touch. So instead, she said, "Look at me, Gabe." Once he complied, she asked, "Hart made you promise you wouldn't touch me?"

He nodded sadly.

"When was this?"

"It was—" He squeezed his eyes closed. "It was at Salamanca."

"On the battlefield?"

"Yes."

There was a roaring in Abbie's ears. "After he had been shot?"

He opened his eyes, and his gaze was tender. "Yes."

"So it was a deathbed promise?" Her voice was rising because that just wasn't cricket, but she forced herself to modulate her tone. "He asked you to make him a deathbed promise?"

"Yes."

"About me?"

"Correct."

As if her brother had the right to make such decisions for her. Had Hart been alive, Abbie would've clouted him right on his pompous head.

No wonder Gabe had been acting so strangely.

Abbie set her jaw. "Tell me what happened."

"You don't want to hear about it, Abbie. Trust me, it was horrible. It was the worst day of my life." He looked down. "I just—I wouldn't want you to feel sad."

Abbie vowed right then and there that one day they would discuss it. She knew Gabe was only trying to protect her, but she was stronger than he realized.

That, and she knew all too well the burden of carrying your sadness all by yourself. Being able to honestly share her struggles with Gabe in her letters had been a godsend.

She was determined to give him the same gift.

But this was not the time to press it. "All right, then. But I insist that you tell me exactly what you said. The exact wording of the promise you made my brother."

Gabe's brow wrinkled. "He asked me to promise that I wouldn't touch you. That I would never lay a hand on you." His eyes were pleading. "That's the only reason I can't do this, Abbie. I would never want you to think there's something wrong with you. There's not. You're beautiful, and desirable, and… and"—he broke off, staring across the room—"everything a man could ever want. But I gave your brother my vow. And I don't mean to break it." He ran a hand over his face. "I'm sorry. I'll return your money. But I can't fulfill the terms of the auction."

Abbie's mind was churning, picking over everything Gabe had just said, and—

Of course.

It was so *obvious.*

She lifted her chin. "There will be no need to return the money."

He shook his head. "I wouldn't feel right accepting it. Not even as a loan. Not after this."

"There is no need for the money to be a loan. I have the perfect solution. You are going to keep your vow to my brother, *and* your promise to make love with me."

"But... but..." Gabe shook his head, looking adorably confused. "That's impossible."

Abbie drew up all her courage and closed the distance between them. They still weren't touching, but their bodies were so close she could feel the heat radiating from his chest. "My brother made you promise you would never touch me," she whispered. "He never said anything about *me* touching *you.*"

CHAPTER 6

Gabe had not heard Abbie correctly.

He knew he hadn't heard her correctly, because the words that had just come out of her mouth were not the kinds of words Actual Abbie said.

To be sure, they were the type of thing the other version of Abbie, Dream Abbie, said all the time.

Gabe had spent *many* hours thinking about Dream Abbie over the past six years. In that brief moment when Hart was dying, when Gabe had thought his friend was asking him to marry his little sister, he had been fairly certain he wanted to marry Abbie.

He had become completely certain he wanted to marry her upon returning to England. It wasn't merely the fact that Abbie had blossomed into a beautiful young woman. She hadn't looked particularly beautiful when he climbed out of the carriage at Pennington House, after all. She'd been blotchy-faced from crying, with red eyes and a dripping nose, and wearing an old black gown of her mother's that fit her like a sack and concealed every one of the delicious curves she had developed in his absence. Even then, something about her had moved him. He'd wanted to scoop her up and go and find a sofa where she could cry on his shoulder for the next hour or the next year or however long it took to make her feel better.

Of course, he'd been able to do none of those things. He'd promised Hart he wouldn't touch her, and the whole reason he was there was to make sure she married another man.

He hadn't meant for his visit to go so badly, but it was impossible to be in the same room with Abbie without wanting to touch her. The only solution was to make sure he was never in the same room with her. He could tell how much his avoidance hurt her, but he didn't know what else he could do. By the day of her wedding, she'd given up on trying to speak to him, and he knew he'd made a hash of everything.

She'd looked so beautiful as she walked down the aisle. Her aunt had prevailed upon her to set aside full mourning for the occasion of her wedding, and she wore a lilac silk gown. There had been no joy in her eyes as she said her vows, but there was a certain poignancy to her beauty intermingled with her sorrow. It had been horrible, watching her walk down that aisle and marry another man, and Gabe had left the second his duty to Hart had been complete.

It was only when he got back to Spain that the extent to which he'd botched everything became apparent. Because, of course, Abbie's letters had been his one source of comfort on the battlefield. With her brother gone, and with him having bungled his visit so spectacularly, there wasn't even a chance she would write.

The six months that followed were probably the darkest of Gabe's life. But then, like a miracle, a letter arrived. Abbie's hurt and anger had almost oozed from the ink, but Gabe hadn't minded. He knew full well he deserved every ounce of ire she hurled at him. And with Abbie safely on the other side of the English Channel, Gabe was able to respond properly, to say all of the things he'd wanted to say the last time he saw her, the things he would've said if he hadn't been so terrified he was going to sweep her up in his arms and never let her go.

But, needless to say, corresponding with wonderful, courageous Abbie, who felt so much and loved so fiercely, had done nothing to quell his suspicion that this was the girl he was meant to marry.

Quite the opposite, in fact.

And so, on those long, lonely nights, alone in his tent, Gabe had allowed himself to dream of her. Dreaming was safe so long as Abbie remained an ocean away.

But now that she was here in the room, he could see that this had been a mistake. There must be something wrong with his brain, because the line between Actual Abbie and Dream Abbie was starting to get all muddled.

Because there was no way Actual Abbie would say *that*.

Gabe cleared his throat. "Would you mind repeating that?"

"You promised that *you* wouldn't touch *me*. But I never promised Hart that *I* would not touch *you*."

He tilted his head to the side and shook it. That was what he'd thought she said, all right. It just didn't make any sense. "I think I misunderstood."

She spoke slowly and deliberately as if she were speaking to a small child. "You promised you would not put your hands on me. You don't have to. I will be the one to put my hands on you."

"I don't think that's what your brother had in mind."

"Well, it's his fault for not being more specific, now isn't it?"

She'd drawn closer to him. He could feel her breath on his

neck, could smell the sweet scent of apricots. "Gabe," she said seductively.

He squeezed his eyes shut to protect himself from the sight of her. "Yes?" he said, his voice tight.

"You know I would never force you into something you didn't want. So if you truly don't want me to touch you, you must tell me so right now."

Say no, he ordered his lips. *Say it right now.*

"No," he gasped. *Good! That was good!* "I do want it."

Wait… he hadn't meant to add that last bit.

Even though it was true.

Add a "but!" his brain demanded.

His lips refused to comply.

And then it was too late because he felt Abbie's fingertips, so soft he almost thought he was dreaming, tracing the contours of his chest. Her thumb stroked his nipple through the thin linen of his shirt, and he shuddered.

His eyes were still closed, so he couldn't see her, but she assaulted his senses nonetheless. With her fingertips, cool and delicate, exploring his chest, his arms. With the sound of pleasure, somewhere between a sigh and a moan, that rose from her throat. With her sweet scent, of honey and apricots and woman, assailing his nose, making him want to lower his lips to her throat to see if she tasted as delectable as she smelled.

Suddenly her hands disappeared, and it was pathetic how bereft Gabe felt without her touch. But then he felt the linen of his shirt shift, and—*dear God*—her petal-soft hands were stroking their way up his bare stomach.

Every muscle in his body was tense under her delicate assault. "Oh!" Abbie gasped, seeming surprised but pleased by what she was discovering beneath his shirt. After exploring the ridges of muscle on his stomach, she slid her hands up and flattened her palms over the planes of his chest. "Would you take off your shirt?"

The garment was fluttering toward the floor before she'd even finished the question.

"*Gabe*." Her voice was full of wonder, and he dared to open his eyes. He was glad he did, because the way Abbie was looking at him, as if he were so magnificent she scarcely had the courage to touch him, was something he would never forget, not if he lived to be as old as Methuselah.

He was desperate to have her hands on him again, and without thinking, raised his hands to frame her face. He froze inches shy of his goal, remembering his vow.

Abbie blew out a startled breath and took his hands in hers. "Come on." She steered him three steps to the side, then pulled the chair out so it wasn't flush against the wall. "Sit there," she said, giving him a playful shove.

Gabe complied, hoping she would climb into his lap, but instead she stepped back. A groan rose in his throat, but then he froze when he realized she was reaching around her back to undo the hooks of her dress.

A flush rose to her cheeks, but she held his eyes the whole time. After a moment of struggling with the fastenings, her bodice sagged open, and then he had to wait the four agonizing seconds it took her to undo the ties of her petticoat before she peeled them off together and deposited them in a heap on the floor.

She stepped out of the garments and kicked them to the side. Her slippers quickly followed. Now she was clad only in her stockings, stays, and a linen shift thin enough that he could tell that she wore no drawers beneath it. She'd chosen a pair of short stays that laced up the front, and Gabe's breath grew ragged as she started picking at the ties with trembling fingers.

The knot gave way, and he watched her work the ties free

from their eyelets. Her breasts were full, the perfect size to fill his hands, and each time she worked a loop free he saw another tantalizing inch of creamy skin through the whisper-thin linen of the shift.

At last, the stays fell open in the front and Abbie shrugged out of them, tossing them to the floor. She glanced up at him, her eyes shy.

What she saw on his face must've reassured her, because her lips slowly curved into a smile. She stalked forward and placed a hand on his shoulder, then, to Gabe's delight, hiked up her shift and climbed into his lap, straddling him.

He was just an inch or two taller than her in this position, and, in addition to stroking her hands up and down his chest, she began kissing her way across his jawline.

Gabe let his head loll back. "I don't know if I can do this."

She froze. "What do you mean? Do—do you want me to stop?"

"God, no. I mean, I don't know if I can keep my hands off you when you're doing *that*."

"Oh!" She glanced him up and down, eyes wide. "If it would help, we could tie your arms to the chair."

He groaned. No, that did not help, not at all. That was the type of thing he had Dream Abbie say to him all the time.

She peered across the room. "Or perhaps it would be better to tie you to the bed."

"You're going to have to tie me to the bed if you keep teasing me like this."

She blinked up at him, her eyes going slightly unfocused. "Is that what I'm doing?" A wicked grin snaked its way across her lips. "Teasing you?"

"Oh, dear. You like that, don't you?"

"Mm-hmm," she murmured, threading her fingers into his hair. Her voice was husky when she whispered, "Let's see how much teasing you can take."

Somehow this seemed like a wonderful idea and a terrible idea in equal measure. He hadn't been with a woman in years. Women weren't exactly thick on the ground when you were on campaign, but in his early years in the army, he'd managed liaisons with a couple of willing widows in Portugal. But Gabe hadn't been with anyone since Hart's death. He'd known nothing could ever come of his feelings for Abbie; he'd just married her off to another man, for Christ's sake. But the prospect of another meaningless encounter had lacked whatever appeal it once held.

Having been without a woman for six years, Gabe would be concerned about his ability to hold out in the least arousing of circumstances.

He chanced a quick glance down, where gorgeous Abbie was squirming in his lap in her whisper-thin shift. This was the opposite of the least arousing of circumstances.

He was in deep, deep trouble.

And it was about to get worse, because Abbie's lips began inching their way up his chin, lingering over his bottom lip before she tilted his head down and kissed him full on the mouth.

It was agony to keep his hands at his side, not to be able to cradle her head, or pull her body flush against his, or run his hands over the beautiful, full breasts that brushed tauntingly against his chest, reminding him that they were just inches away. Abbie's kisses were eager, yet tentative, as if she wasn't sure quite what to do. Considering her only experience with kissing, as far as he knew, was with Dulson, it was perhaps unsurprising that she hadn't learned much in the way of technique.

But Gabe had enough technique for the both of them, and so he took charge, tilting his head to the side and sweeping his tongue across her lips. She hesitated just a beat before opening for him. As he caressed the rim of her lips with his tongue, she made a sound of surprised pleasure. She began copying his motions, timidly at first, but with growing confidence, especially after he growled his approval into her mouth, and soon their tongues were tangling deliciously.

Abbie's motions were growing more frantic. Her hands scrambled against his chest, slid over his shoulders and down his back, causing her breasts to press against him. She seemed to enjoy the contact, for she made a mewling sound and began undulating against his torso, which was the most exquisite kind of torture. But she didn't move to press her sensitive core against his cock, which was perfectly positioned for her to take her pleasure. This made Gabe wonder if she knew about the little pearl between her legs.

He flexed his hips, rubbing her there, and she froze. Slowly she lifted her gaze to him, her eyes glassy. He began circling his hips and she cried out, burying her face in his neck.

"No. Look at me, Abbie." He nudged her with his shoulder, and she raised her head. Her face was intoxicated with pleasure. "That's right, love. Let me see it. Let me see what I'm doing to you."

"Oh, Gabe, that's—that feels so… so…"

He used his knees to nudge her legs farther apart as he continued to rock against her, and she cried out again. "Tell me how it feels," he demanded.

"So good," she gasped. She'd picked up the rhythm and was now riding him, setting the pace she desired and experimenting with different angles until she found the one that pleased her most. Her nails dug into his shoulders, and the pain made his pleasure all the more piquant.

His cock flexed its approval, and Abbie laughed. "You like this, too, don't you?"

"God, yes." He bent his head and began kissing her neck.

He tried not to leave marks all over her petal-soft skin, but he was so far gone he wasn't sure he would succeed.

"Ooooh, Gabe! That feels good, too!" She gave a breathless chuckle. "I thought I was supposed to be the one teasing you."

"You are." He brought his lips up to lave her ear. "Believe me, you are."

Her eyes had taken on a mischievous glint. When she spoke, her voice was husky. "But I'll bet I could tease you even more."

She scooted back, which caused him to whimper in protest. *God*, how his hands itched to cup those full, round, perfect breasts. "Please, Abbie—"

He wasn't sure what he was going to ask her to do, but it didn't matter. The words died on his lips as he realized what she intended.

Her hands had reached down to the front of his pantaloons. Her fingers were fumbling with the buttons of his falls.

The pads of her fingers rubbed the head of his cock as she worked the button directly on top of it, and his head fell back on a moan.

Abbie froze, misinterpreting the feral sound he had made. "Is—is that all right?"

"It's more than all right," he hastened to reassure her.

"You like that, then?" she asked, abandoning the button and instead stroking her sweet little hand up and down his length, caressing him through his pantaloons.

His thoughts turned to scrambled eggs because Gabe knew his body well enough to realize that he was seconds away from spending right in his trousers. The pleasure was exquisite, and he wanted to come desperately, but—but—

His hand shot out and grasped Abbie's around the wrist, pulling her hand away from his straining cock.

This was not how he wanted it to be.

When he came, he wanted to be inside her.

They both stared at their joined hands, reveling in the significance that he had broken, that *he* had touched *her*.

He was breathing hard, but he managed to get a few words out. "Shift off. On the bed. *Now*."

CHAPTER 7

Abbie had never been naked in front of a man before.

It was a strange thing for a woman who had been married and widowed, but it was true. When she'd lain with Dulson, it had usually been dark, and mostly he just drew her shift up rather than undress her fully.

The hotel suite, on the other hand, was bright with beeswax candles. As she knelt on the bed, Abbie felt a pang of nerves, wondering if Gabe would find her attractive. But she forced herself to meet his eye as she drew her shift up over her head and tossed it aside, leaving her in nothing but black silk stockings held up by black ribboned garters.

He froze, and the heat in his eyes as his gaze raked up and down her body helped her to relax a fraction. He stalked over to the bed, not even tearing his eyes from her as he kicked off his boots. "On your back," he growled.

Abbie sank back onto the plush white counterpane, and —*merciful heavens*—Gabe crawled right on top of her. Her body jolted at the delicious feeling of all his satiny, golden skin brushing against hers.

To say that he kissed her next would be the most pallid

sort of understatement. He did not kiss so much as devour. This was the moment Abbie determined that Gabe's reputation as the most skillful lover in all of England wasn't mere hyperbole. Never had she imagined that a mere kiss could produce such exquisite sensations, but within seconds, he had her desperate for him, clinging to his shoulders and making sounds she hadn't realized herself capable of. Her heart began to pound, and her thighs began to tremble, and then her heart began to pound *between* her thighs, which didn't even make sense, except it was happening.

All the while, Gabe's hands remained fisted in the bedclothes, his grip so tight that veins stood out along his forearms.

He ripped his lips from hers with a growl and began kissing his way down her neck.

"G-Gabe!" she gasped. "I—I need…"

Abbie broke off, as she wasn't actually sure what she needed, but Gabe made soothing sounds as he pressed his lips against her clavicle, then trailed them lower, over the upper swell of her breast. "Don't worry, darling. I know what you need."

He brushed a gentle kiss against her nipple, which was *wonderful,* but then he pulled back, which was *excruciating.* Abbie cried out in frustration. He proceeded to torture her, kissing every inch of her breast other than the spot where she wanted his lips most desperately.

At last, when he teased the edge of her areola for the third time, she grabbed him by the back of his head and pressed her nipple into his mouth. He made a sound of approval as he gave her the strong suction she'd been craving, and she cried out, her hips bucking upon the bed.

Unthinkingly, he reached a hand out to cup her other breast, then froze, realizing what he'd been about to do. His wrist flexed in midair, and his chest turned to iron above her as he struggled for control.

As he started to return his trembling hand to the counterpane, Abbie caught him by the wrist. "No, Gabe."

"But, Abbie, I promised. I promised your brother I wouldn't—"

She ran her thumb over his lips. "Hush. I don't want to hear what you promised my brother. It doesn't matter, anyway."

His breath was ragged. "It matters to me."

"You will not be putting your hands on me. *I* will be putting your hands on me. Because that is where I want them." She took his hand and guided it to her breast. As reluctant as he'd been, he moaned, and couldn't resist palming her fullness.

She caressed his face, forcing him to look at her. "Hart had no right to ask that of you. I'm his sister, not his property. The only person who has any say in who gets to touch me is *me*. And if we are only to have this one night together, I want absolutely everything you can give me."

Gabe's face looked pained, but he nodded, cradled her face in his hands, and kissed her.

After having denied himself for so long, Gabe couldn't seem to get enough of her. His hands were everywhere, and —*oh*! Unfettering him had been *the best* decision, because *gracious heavens*, Gabriel Davenport was good with his hands. Abbie would not have thought that having her nipple pinched would be pleasurable, but it felt exquisite, almost unbearably so.

Gabe broke off their kiss and began working his way down her body. He groaned at the sight of her breasts filling his hands but didn't stop touching her. "I'm going to hell."

"No, you're not," Abbie protested.

"It will be worth it," he murmured before his lips closed over her nipple.

While he worshipped her there, his hands continued their explorations, caressing her neck, finding a sensitive spot behind her ear, then creating a shower of pins as he threaded his fingers into her hair so he could massage her scalp. All the while, his mouth teased one nipple and then the other, and he soon had her writhing on the bed, all but sobbing with a potent mix of pleasure and unmet need.

The only problem was that Abbie had no idea what it was that she needed. She had never felt this way before. But she felt quite certain that if she didn't get this *thing*, whatever it was, she would *die*.

Just when she was on the cusp of begging him to help her, his hands drifted down her body, past her breasts, across her stomach, which was rising and falling in fast pants, then over her hips.

He caressed her thighs, then pressed them open. She was far beyond the point at which she might feel embarrassed to have him gazing upon her most intimate spot. Being here, naked in Gabe's arms felt like the most natural thing in the world.

"*God, Abbie.*" His eyes were fixed upon the juncture of her thighs, rapt. He leaned forward and breathed in. "You even smell like heaven. You can't know how I've dreamed of this."

"You—you have?" she asked breathlessly. "I never imagined you thought of me this way."

He pressed a kiss to the inside of her thigh. "That's what I wanted you to think. But the truth is, I've dreamed of this moment a thousand times—the moment when I finally taste you."

"Oh, Gabe, I've dreamed of this moment—*wait.*" She frowned, rising onto one elbow. "What do you mean, *taste* me?"

He paused from trailing kisses up the inside of her thigh. "You said earlier that you wanted everything I could give you."

"I… I do."

He looked up at her, his green eyes sparkling in the candlelight. "Do you trust me?"

"Well, yes." She could feel the heat rising in her cheeks. "But surely you don't mean to kiss me on my, um…"

"Let me show you." He brought one thumb to her core and delved between her most intimate folds. Finding the spot he sought, he began gently circling his thumb. Abbie stilled.

It felt… she wasn't sure how it felt. It felt almost… *too* good. Because surely it wasn't right, the way her legs were trembling, the unladylike sheen of sweat that had broken out across her chest, and the urge to crawl out of her own skin.

Gabe's gaze was knowing. "You feel that."

Abbie couldn't seem to stop squirming, so urgent were these strange sensations. "I—I'm not sure. It feels good, but am I supposed to feel… desperate?"

"That's *exactly* how you're supposed to feel." And with that, Gabe replaced his thumb with his *mouth*, and oh! That felt decadent and wicked, like eating bonbons for dinner. Now there was no hope that Abbie could lie motionless on the bed. Gabe brought his hands to her hips so he could hold her still enough to pleasure her.

He started with teasing flicks with the tip of his tongue, studying her closely all the while to gauge her reaction. As the storm within Abbie built, his pace quickened, as did the pressure he used, so that by the time she was crying out mindlessly, he was laving her with the flat of his tongue.

Just when Abbie thought she could not possibly bear any more, he sealed his lips over the little knob that was the center of these beautiful sensations and started to suck. And as her thighs began to shake and she bit her own wrist to keep from screaming, Abbie knew instinctively that this was it, this was *the thing* that everyone talked about. Divine pleasure overwhelmed her like a river flooding its banks, a sensation that was simultaneously the best and worst thing that had ever happened to her. The best for obvious reasons, but the worst because this would be her one and only night with Gabe, and she knew she would never experience anything like this ever again.

Her eyes were closed, and she was still only marginally aware of her surroundings when she felt Gabe come up beside her and take her into his arms. He was so warm, and his skin was surprisingly soft, like satin over the hard planes of his muscular frame. And pressing into her stomach, there was steel.

Abbie found herself overwhelmed by this, the sign of Gabe's still urgent need. She wanted to give him the same exquisite pleasure he had just bestowed upon her. She rolled onto her back, tugging at his shoulders, encouraging him to follow her. He instead rose and unbuttoned the falls of his pantaloons so roughly she was surprised the fabric didn't rend.

Once the pantaloons were in a heap on the floor, he reached for the glass of water on the nightstand and fished out one of the translucent sheaths floating inside. Abbie watched him slide it over his straining shaft, which was significantly larger than her husband's had been, and felt a pang of nerves. The lovemaking act had been uncomfortable enough with George. What if she simply wasn't cut out for this kind of thing, in spite of Gabe's legendary skill? She was still determined to try, but she found herself feeling uncertain, in spite of the pleasure he had given her moments ago.

Gabe secured the ribbon with surprising speed, given how much his hands were shaking. Grabbing one of the folded hand towels, he dabbed off the excess moisture, then took up the bottle of oil and poured a few drops onto his palm. His gaze roamed hungrily across Abbie's naked body as he smoothed the oil up and down his length. She could see the pleasure in his eyes as he stroked his own cock, and heat rose in her cheeks.

Much to Abbie's surprise, instead of entering her at once, the way George would have done, Gabe reached up and seized one of the pillows. He folded it in half and carefully positioned it beneath her hips.

It was on the tip of her tongue to ask what he was doing when Gabe slowly began to slide inside her. That was when she realized just how different tonight was from her prior lovemaking experiences. Thanks to the pleasure he had given her earlier, everything between her legs was deliciously slick, and much to her wonder, she felt no discomfort, none at all, even as he seated himself to the hilt. Slowly, lifting his head so he could watch her the whole time, he began sliding in and out.

Abbie had never much enjoyed this portion of lovemaking—or any portion, truth be told—at least, when her partner had been her deceased husband. But this felt… different. Maybe it was Gabe's gorgeous body lying atop hers, perfect beneath her fingertips. Maybe it was the fact that her body was already humming with desire. Or maybe it was the angle created by the pillow.

But Gabe's cock sliding in and out of her felt *interesting* in a way she had never experienced before.

She glanced up to find him studying her intently. A vein popped out on his forehead as he shifted his weight backward. Suddenly Abbie's hands were grasping fistfuls of the bedclothes. Because that spot he was rubbing against, that felt… that felt…

A wolfish grin snaked its way across Gabe's face. "Aha, there it is."

Abbie's breath was coming in pants. "There's… there's what?"

"The spot I was looking for." Gabe rocked back another inch as he continued his thrusts, and Abbie gasped in pleasure.

The sensations built and built, a beautiful tide rising within her, the anticipation of it spilling over exquisite.

But then, Gabe surprised her by threading a hand between their bodies. "Gabe?" she asked as his warm palm slid across her stomach. "What are you d-do… *Oh.*"

Her head fell back as his fingers again found that magical spot between her legs, the same one he had used to bring her such exquisite pleasure earlier. All the while, he continued thrusting inside of her, and the combination was devastating. She lasted mere seconds before another climax overwhelmed her. Never had Abbie felt so out of control of her body as she was wracked with wave after unrelenting wave of pleasure, her body shaking like a rag doll upon the bed.

On the edge of her consciousness, she became aware of his strokes growing faster, more frantic. And then his body hardened to iron atop hers, and he cried out as he spasmed inside her.

Gabe collapsed on top of her, burying his face in the pillow next to hers. She stroked her fingers over the smooth skin of his back, which was slick with the barest sheen of sweat.

After a moment, Gabe raised his head and kissed her tenderly, then settled beside her, cradling her head upon his shoulder.

After a few minutes, Gabe's heartbeat slowed beneath her ear. Abbie gave him a squeeze. "Well, that was worth every penny."

The rumble of Gabe's chuckle filled her ear. "Good. I just wish…"

He trailed off as if remembering himself. But Abbie suspected she knew what he had almost said—that he wished this would not be their only night together.

She felt precisely the same way. But it was impossible. He needed a great heiress.

And, barring a great miracle, she was going to have to marry her tormentor, Nigel Davies.

Gabe cleared his throat. "So, I think your latest letter and I must've passed each other in the night. Literally. How have you been?"

Abbie traced her hand over the firm planes of his chest, considering her answer. A part of her didn't want to waste a second of their one and only night together on sad thoughts.

But this was Gabe, her last remaining confidant, and the temptation to unburden herself after months of carrying her problems alone was even stronger.

"Not so well, truth be told. Did you receive the letter I sent you in May? The one that mentioned the papers I found in the attic of the dower house?"

"The ones belonging to Carlotta de Noronha? Of course." He rubbed her shoulder. "How did old Nigel take the news?"

Abbie settled her head more comfortably on his shoulder. "Even worse than I feared. You see…"

CHAPTER 8

Lymington, Hampshire
April 1818
Three Months Earlier

ABBIE FOUND the diary on a high shelf in the library, tucked so far back it was hidden from ground level.

She had recently undertaken a project: sorting through the decades of detritus left behind in the dower house by the Ladies Dulson who had come before her. It was a way to pass the time. Society considered it unseemly for widows to attend large parties and gatherings during their first year of mourning, so Abbie's only option was to socialize quietly with her own relations. Unfortunately, this limited her circle to Uncle Edmond's family and George's cousin, Nigel, and it was difficult to say whose company held less appeal.

Most of what she found held little interest—old lists, rusty hairpins, and moth-eaten bonnets. But when she placed her hand upon the journal, a curious tingle ran down her arm. She was struck by a sudden feeling that at last, she had found something interesting, even before she pulled it from the shelf.

It proved to be a journal, handsomely bound in reddish-brown leather. When she opened it, she discovered that it had been written in Portuguese.

It happened that Abbie could read Portuguese. She'd always had an affinity for languages, and her French had been better than her brother's when she was nine and he fifteen. When Hart decided to join the army, Abbie suggested they study Portuguese together, knowing that she could help him along. She continued her studies even after he departed for Portugal. It was a way for her to feel close to her brother even when they were leagues apart.

The journal had been written around sixty-five years ago by a woman named Carlotta de Noronha. Abbie was familiar enough with the family history to know that Carlotta had been the third Baroness Dulson, married briefly to George and Nigel's great-uncle. Her husband died of a fever just a few months after their wedding. The union had not produced any children, so the barony had passed to George and Nigel's grandfather.

Carlotta's journal was a delight. She had a sardonic wit and a droll turn of phrase. Abbie quickly came to understand that Carlotta had found her own Lord Dulson about as stimulating as Abbie had found George—which was to say, not at all.

But that was where the similarities ended. After having lost her parents and brother in such quick succession, being forced to marry a man she didn't love, and finding herself a widow by the age of twenty-four, perhaps it was understandable that Abbie felt beaten down and resigned to a quiet, dreary future.

Carlotta, on the other hand, regarded her widowhood as a new dawn. She immediately took a lover—one of the stable hands, an unimaginable scandal—ordered a more daring wardrobe, and began making plans to tour the Continent just as soon as her affairs on the English side of the channel could be brought in order.

It seemed that this process did not go the way Carlotta hoped. She wasn't the most regular diarist, sometimes filling a dozen pages in one day, and sometimes recording nothing for weeks. But Abbie was able to glean through the gaps that there was some sort of dispute about Carlotta's dowry, which included three hundred acres of prime wine country back in Portugal's Douro Valley. Oftentimes marriage settlements were structured such that if the husband died without issue, the dowry assets would revert to the widow or her family. In this case, though, the judge ruled that the vineyards would remain part of the Dulson estate.

Carlotta had disagreed. *Vehemently.* She cursed the day she married Lord Dulson and decamped for the Continent, leaving her journal behind in her haste.

Having been part of the Davies family for five years, Abbie was aware of the family lore that Carlotta had spent the next fifty years crisscrossing Europe, always leaving scandals in her wake. Ironically, despite her efforts to bid them good riddance, Carlotta was buried in the Davies family plot, as she had died at the age of seventy-six in a moment that her travels had happened to bring her to London. As she was technically still Lady Dulson, someone had suggested her body be brought to Hampshire and interred in the family plot at St. Thomas's Church, and although the Davies did not harbor any fondness for this particular Lady Dulson, denying her a somewhat-dignified burial would mean a loss of face they were not willing to countenance. So that was how Carlotta de Noronha came to be buried next to a man she despised in a place she had fled at the first opportunity.

After she started reading Carlotta's journal, Abbie used to visit her grave sometimes. She honestly thought of Carlotta as a friend, just about the only one she had, truth be told. Abbie knew it was foolish, but she had been so lonely during her year of mourning, and it was difficult to understate the impact Carlotta's journal had upon her. Reading it awakened something inside of her, something that had been lying dormant since her parents' deaths. She didn't feel lively, precisely. But, for the first time in six years, she could remember what it had felt like when she had been a carefree young girl. And she felt such a kinship with Carlotta, her fellow Lady Dulson, who had risen above the lot life had handed her and forged her own path, one full of adventure and passion.

Abbie was just starting to wonder if she could perhaps do the same when she found that fateful box in the attic of the dower house.

Having finished organizing the main rooms of the house, Abbie had moved on to the attic. The box in question looked ordinary enough, and upon opening it, Abbie had discovered a cache of papers belonging to Carlotta. Most of them were mundane—receipts from the haberdasher's shop in Lymington, or recipes for Portuguese delicacies such as *Bacalhau à Lagareiro*, with a note scrawled in the margin in which Carlotta insisted that her cook use the full recommended amount of garlic, adding, *What exactly are you afraid of, that it will taste good?*

Some of the papers looked more official—legal documents, perhaps. Nothing as interesting as Carlotta's diary, much to Abbie's regret. She had to break off before she could inspect everything as she had received an invitation to dine with her uncle's family at her former home, Pennington House, and it was time to dress for dinner.

Nigel Davies was also in attendance that evening. Abbie's

cousins dominated the conversation, chattering about the upcoming London Season—the dresses they would order, the balls they would attend, and the bonnets they had trimmed in preparation.

Nobody asked Abbie how she was faring. It was not until the dessert course when her cousins were tucking into their strawberry ices that Abbie found an opening in the conversation.

"I found something of interest when I was sorting through the attic today," she announced.

"Oh?" Aunt Priscilla did not trouble to look up from her ice as she responded, nor did she infuse her voice with anything resembling interest.

"It was a box of papers," Abbie continued, undeterred. She was used to this reception at her aunt and uncle's home. "Most of them were just old receipts and recipes, but—"

"Are there any macarons?" her cousin Beatrice interrupted. "I'm so sick of ices. We've had them *twice* this week."

"Ices are Lord Dulson's favorite," Aunt Priscilla said, offering Nigel a simpering smile. Abbie knew her aunt hoped to marry one of her five daughters off to the new baron, even though Nigel seemed to have inherited all of George's bad qualities (drabness and lack of imagination), and none of his good ones (kindness and fundamental decency). They were welcome to him, as far as Abbie was concerned.

Beatrice gave a petulant huff, and silence resumed at the table. Abbie decided to try again. "So, the papers I mentioned —most of them were just household records. But I was excited to discover them because they belonged to the former Carlotta de Noronha."

From across the table came the clang of a spoon hitting the floor. Abbie glanced up, startled, to see that Nigel had overturned the porcelain cup containing his strawberry ice.

Nigel righted the cup and accepted a new spoon from a footman. "Papers belonging to Carlotta de Noronha, you say?"

"Y-yes." Although Abbie had never much liked Nigel, she'd always thought him harmless enough.

But now, something about the way Nigel's weaselly eyes bore into hers caused a shiver to run down her spine.

Nigel's knuckles were white where he gripped his new spoon. "You said *most* of them were household records."

"Th-that's correct."

"What were the other ones?"

"I couldn't honestly say. I only discovered the box this afternoon and have yet to sort through its contents in detail."

"Were there any legal records?" Nigel asked nonchalantly, but his fingers were clumsy as he attempted to scoop up a bite of strawberry ice, and the spoon clattered against the side of the cup. He hastily set the dessert aside.

"It's possible. I only had time to give them the barest glance."

"I see," Nigel said shortly. "Do let me know if you should find anything of interest."

He did not speak to her for the rest of the night, but several times Abbie caught him watching her from across the room. He glanced away quickly, but each time, Abbie felt her stomach perform a nauseating flip.

She felt so unnerved that even though it was eleven o'clock when she arrived home, she waved off her maid's offer to help her undress and went straight to the parlor where she'd left the box. Shuffling through the papers by lamplight, it didn't take long to find the legal document to which Nigel had been alluding: a copy of Carlotta's marriage contract.

Abbie didn't have any legal training. But the contract was clear enough: in the event that her husband died without issue, Carlotta's dowry, including the vineyards in the Douro Valley and three thousand pounds' worth of stock in the Bank of England, would revert to her.

Abbie didn't know what had happened to the bank stock. But she knew of a certainty that those vineyards were now part of the Dulson estate.

Which begged the question—why was Nigel so perturbed by Abbie finding a box of Carlotta's old records? Clearly, Carlotta had disagreed with the judge's ruling, and there did appear to be some evidence that she should have retained her family's vineyards. But in the end, the Davies had won and Carlotta had lost, and after sixty years, surely the judge's ruling was now final.

Unless…

Abbie was no legal expert. But, as far as she knew, one of the few ways a prior ruling could be overturned was if the verdict had been obtained through fraud.

Nigel's strained reaction suggested he had something to hide. The question was, what?

She peered at the signature of the attorney who had prepared the contract. *Collingsworth.* A name she recognized well—the Collingsworth family had run a solicitor's office in the nearby town of Lymington for three generations. Mr. John Collingsworth, the current managing partner, had been her father's own attorney.

Perhaps Mr. Collingsworth could shed some light on this apparent discrepancy.

$\mathcal{A}$bbie awoke the next morning with a tightness in her chest. She dressed hastily and choked down a little tea and toast before setting out for Lymington. She selected one of her larger reticules, one that was big enough to hold a book, and inside she tucked both Carlotta's marriage contract and her most recent letter to Gabe, which she intended to post while she was in town.

The morning was clear and bright, so Abbie decided to make the one-mile journey on foot. A bell chimed as she opened the door to Collingsworth and Collingsworth.

As the Earl of Pennington's daughter and Baron Dulson's wife, Abbie was well-known around town, and a clerk rose to greet her with a bow. "Lady Dulson, how may I be of assistance?"

"I wondered if Mr. Collingsworth could spare a moment to speak with me."

"I feel certain that he will," the clerk said, ushering her toward one of the back offices.

Inside, she found not only John Collingsworth but his father, Leopold, who was now retired from the family business. The senior Mr. Collingsworth rose from his chair and clasped her hands in his wrinkled ones. "Lady Dulson, what a treat! I certainly picked the right day to visit the offices."

Abbie pressed his hand. "The pleasure is mine." She settled into the chair the younger Mr. Collingsworth brought over for her. "Thank you so much for making time to see me today."

"Of course," John Collingsworth said, seating himself behind his desk. "How may we be of assistance, my lady?"

Abbie had intended to show Mr. Collingsworth Carlotta's marriage contract, but now that she was here, she found herself hesitating. Gracious, but Nigel had her feeling skittish! She knew she was probably being ridiculous but opted to err on the side of caution. "I believe you, or rather, your firm, drew up the marriage contract between one of my predecessors as Lady Dulson, Carlotta de Noronha, and the fourth baron. Is that correct?"

"It very well might be," John Collingsworth said. "Our firm has handled the baron's business for many a year. Although that would have been well before my time."

"It's correct," Leopold offered from his chair along the wall. "My father was the one to draw it up. It was one of the last things he did before his untimely passing. A sudden apoplexy, it was," he explained, patting his chest.

"I'm so sorry for your loss," Abbie murmured.

"Thank you, my lady," Leopold said.

"May I inquire as to the reason for your interest?" John asked.

"Yes, I—I've been going through the dower house, trying to organize the contents. And I found some, um… some old jewelry in a box in the attic," Abbie improvised. "Nothing valuable, mind you. Two necklaces and a brooch. But based on the style, I thought they might have belonged to Carlotta, and I wondered if the marriage contract mentioned any jewelry she brought with her to her marriage."

"Let's see, shall we?" John opened a drawer in one of the cabinets that lined the walls and began leafing through its folders.

"It's not terribly important," Abbie babbled nervously. "Just a bit of family history."

"Of course," Leopold said. "And these sorts of things are often mentioned in marriage contracts. It's not uncommon for them to specify that a bride is to retain possession of her personal jewelry."

John had slid a folder from the drawer and was flipping through the pages. "Here it is," he said, laying the folder upon the desk. He scanned the document, which was three pages long. "Although I don't see a mention of any jewelry."

"Would you mind if I had a look?" Abbie tried to make her voice serene even as her heart threatened to pound right out of her chest.

"Not at all." John turned the document to face her and indicated a particular paragraph on the top page. "This is the portion that lists the assets Carlotta brought to her marriage. There are some vineyards in Portugal, and three thousand pounds' worth of stock in the Bank of England, with the specification that half of the interest produced each year is to be re-invested in stock." He gave a low whistle. "That would be worth a handsome fortune today. But I do not see mention of any jewelry."

Abbie pulled the document close enough to read. She barely skimmed the paragraph listing Carlotta's assets, which appeared to be identical to the document she'd found in the attic. It was the paragraph below, the one that detailed the disbursement of those assets should the marriage not produce any children, upon which she fixed her attention.

Surely enough, the words, "shall be returned to Miss de

Noronha" had been replaced with, "shall be retained by the Dulson estate."

Abbie sagged back in her chair and found the two Mr. Collingsworths regarding her quizzically. Straightening, she forced a breezy smile. "I cannot say I am surprised these pieces were not mentioned. As I said, they do not appear to be of great value. But it was worth a try."

"Of course, my lady," John said.

"Well." Abbie's fingers trembled as she gathered up the pages of the contract. "I'll have to find another method by which to determine—oh, bother," she said as she fumbled the bottom two sheets, which went fluttering to the floor.

"Allow me, my lady," Leopold said, starting to rise from his chair.

She wasn't about to make an eighty-year-old man bend down to get them. "Oh, no. Please, let me." She scooped them easily off the floor. "After all, it was due to my clumsiness that… that…"

She trailed off as her eyes fell upon the final page of the contract.

The one that bore Carlotta's signature.

Or, to be more accurate, the one that bore Carlotta's name. Because although someone had scrawled *Carlotta de Noronha* on the appropriate line, that was *not* Carlotta's signature.

Abbie would know. She was reading her diary, after all.

Cold dread pooled inside her stomach. Now that she looked at the signature of the Mr. Collingsworth who had completed this document, it, too, did not match the copy she had neatly folded in her reticule.

The signatures had been forged. Abbie was certain of it.

Every piece of evidence pointed to the fact that someone had conspired to deprive Carlotta of her dowry. Including…

Abbie blinked at the two Misters Collingsworth, who

were once again regarding her with a sort of kindhearted befuddlement. She did not like to think that either of them was involved; these men had dutifully looked after her family's interests for generations. But the fact remained that someone had removed the true contract from that file and replaced it with the forgery.

Although now that she thought on it, that did not necessarily mean that either Mr. Collingsworth had been involved. Whatever clerks they had employed sixty-five years ago would have had access to the files, and the fact that they had produced the contract for her to inspect without the slightest hesitation suggested that they had nothing to hide.

Then there was the fact that Leopold's father, who would have been familiar with the terms of the contract and who would have known at once that those terms had been altered, had happened to die shortly after the agreement was signed. That event had created an opportunity that someone had seized upon.

It wasn't difficult to guess whom. One family had benefited from the changes that were made.

The Davies.

She became aware that John Collingsworth was speaking. "My lady? My lady, is everything all right?"

She hastily set the contract on the desk. "Yes. My apologies, gentlemen. I was just... woolgathering." She stood. "Thank you both for your time today."

Outside, Abbie hurried down High Street to the local posting inn, The Angel. Inside, she begged the barmaid, Maggie, for pen and ink, and scrawled a quick postscript on Gabe's letter, advising him about the box of documents and her suspicions that Carlotta's marriage contract had been falsified. Then she gave it to Maggie to be posted.

She made her way home in a trance, turning the facts over again and again.

She was so lost in thought that she almost plowed into the saddle horse tied to her front gate.

Immediately she felt queasy because she recognized that horse.

It belonged to Nigel.

Some strange impulse had her ducking behind a tree, folding Carlotta's marriage contract into quarters, and tucking the sheets inside her stays, rather than leaving them in her reticule. Once she was satisfied that the folded paper was not discernible, she emerged from behind the tree and strode through her front door.

She heard raised voices from the parlor where Abbie had taken the box. Peering around the doorframe, she saw her housekeeper, Mrs. Brownlee, wringing her hands. "Beggin' yer pardon, m'lord. But I think ye should wait until Lady Dulson returns."

Nigel's voice held a note of exasperation. He was already leafing through the papers in the box. "Lady Dulson will not mind. Now leave."

Abbie stepped into the room, striving to keep her voice from shaking. "Nigel, what on earth are you doing?"

He spun around, his expression holding more annoyance than guilt. "I have come to inspect the papers you mentioned last night. Any legal papers relating to Carlotta de Noronha are the business of the estate and would have been placed here by accident."

Abbie crossed her arms. "Carlotta de Noronha had a life, and business dealings, both before and after her tenure as Lady Dulson. So what you say is not necessarily the case. But this is my home, and I do not appreciate you inviting yourself inside to sift through my belongings. You have overstepped. Badly."

Abbie saw something flicker in his eyes, something dark

and angry. He stalked across the room toward her. "You speak as if you have something to hide."

Abbie had to stop herself from taking a step back. "Don't be ridiculous."

He stopped just in front of her. "Let's see, shall we?"

To Abbie's shock, he reached out and seized her reticule.

"Nigel!" She pursued him across the room to the table where the box of documents rested and watched him unceremoniously dump the contents of her reticule across the glossy cherrywood surface. "This is outrageous!"

Finding nothing more interesting than some hair pins, a handkerchief, and Hart's battered pocket watch, Nigel scowled.

"Are you satisfied?" Abbie snapped, snatching her fan, which was teetering on the edge of the table. "What a disgraceful thing to have done!"

Nigel showed no sign of remorse. "Well, I had to be sure, now, didn't I?"

Abbie drew herself up with every ounce of dignity she possessed. When she spoke, her voice shook not with fear, but with ire. "I must insist that you leave. Immediately."

The corners of Nigel's lips tipped up, but not in a nice way. "Certainly. But"—he seized the box of papers—"I'll be taking this with me."

"You most certainly will not!" Abbie chased after him as he strode toward the door. Spying her lone footman lingering by the front door, she cried, "Brett, stop him!"

Brett was a strapping young man, four inches taller than Nigel and sufficiently broad of shoulder that he was normally well up to the task of deterring potential intruders. But he allowed Nigel to pass.

He turned to Abbie, his eyes miserable. "I'm sorry, my lady. But I can't lay hands upon the baron."

Abbie sighed. Brett was right, of course. Nigel might be

entirely in the wrong, but no doubt he could make life a misery for a mere servant who dared to manhandle him.

"It's all right," Abbie said. "It doesn't much matter that he took that box. He'll quickly come to discover that all it contains are old shopping lists and recipes for roast octopus."

"Still," Mrs. Brownlee huffed, coming to stand behind Abbie and glaring at Nigel's back as he rode away, "it's the principle of the matter."

"Precisely," Abbie said, shutting the front door and turning the key.

She spent the rest of the day putting on a good show for her household staff.

But Abbie knew the truth—she had come within a hairsbreadth of disaster. It turned out that her instinct to hide Carlotta's marriage contract inside her corset hadn't been an overreaction after all.

Nigel would be back. Abbie felt sure of it.

And when he came, she was going to be prepared.

CHAPTER 10

 igel did not keep her in suspense. The following day, he pounded on her door before Abbie had even finished her soft-boiled egg.

After his abominable behavior the previous day, Abbie wasn't about to let Nigel back inside her house, so she stepped onto her little front porch to confront him.

He had brought the box of Carlotta's documents with him. Scowling, he thrust it into her hands.

"Nigel," she said crisply, accepting the box and setting it down next to the door. "I wish I could say it was a pleasure. I trust you have satisfied yourself that whatever legal papers you sought, they were not present."

"Where is it?" he asked, his words imbued with quiet menace.

"I don't know what you're talking about," Abbie lied, ignoring the fact that the document to which he referred was at that very moment digging into the underside of her left breast.

"Quit lying!" Nigel snarled. "Do you think I don't know about your little trip to town yesterday?"

Abbie lifted her chin. "I was posting a letter. You may ask Maggie at The Angel Inn—"

"My man saw you go into the Angel. But before that, he saw you enter the office of Collingsworth and Collingsworth."

She bit her lower lip to stop it from quivering. "Why should that come as a surprise? The Collingsworths have handled my family's business for generations. It is only natural that I use them for my own legal affairs."

"Those forthright old fools have already given you up!" Nigel snapped. "All I had to do was walk in there, sit down for a chat, mention your name on the barest pretext, and they promptly told me all about your visit. It was child's play to get them to reveal every detail. So you may stop playing dumb because I already know you asked to see Carlotta's marriage contract. Such a coincidence, the day after you found a box of her old papers."

"And why," Abbie ground out, her voice shaking, "should it worry you if I ask about Carlotta's marriage contract? Unless you have something to hide?"

With a snarl, Nigel grabbed her arm and dragged her away from the house.

"Let me go!" Abbie shrieked, struggling to find her pocket slit so she could reach the item she'd carefully concealed beneath her skirts.

"Oh, calm down," Nigel said, releasing her abruptly once they reached the same oak tree Abbie had ducked behind yesterday. "It's obvious you've seen that other copy of the marriage contract. The one, might I add, that was found by the High Court to be a fraud."

Abbie found herself speechless. She was shocked that Nigel was laying his cards out on the table in such a flagrant manner.

But she noted his careful wording—that the court had *ruled* the contract in Abbie's possession to be fraudulent.

That didn't mean it *was* a fraud. Based on the signatures, Abbie was convinced hers was the true copy.

Nigel held out a hand, palm side up. "Now quit wasting time and give it here."

Abbie swallowed. Nigel knew too much for her to play dumb. But she hadn't considered that the conversation would take this turn, and she hadn't had time to think through what she was going to say. "If the high court has already ruled this other document a fraud, then why are you so concerned about its existence?" Nigel did not respond, so she continued, "I think it's because you know the truth. The document I found bears Carlotta's signature. The one ratified by the high court does not. Admit it, Nigel. We both know which copy is the fraud."

"It was for the high court to determine which one was a fraud! Their ruling is final."

"That may be true. Although I think the case might be re-opened should new evidence be discovered." Abbie started, as a new approach occurred to her. "If any fraud was committed, it was done before either of us was born. You are blameless in this, Nigel. I know you must be worried that this document coming to light might cause a scandal, or tarnish the memory of your grandfather, but—"

Nigel's laugh was derisive. "Tarnish the memory of my grandfather? As if I cared about that. Do you have any idea how much those vineyards bring in every year? More than half of my income!"

Abbie sighed. So much for her attempts to ascribe nobler impulses to Nigel Davies.

Nigel made a slashing motion with his hand. "The vineyards will be staying with the Dulson estate. Now, give me that contract!"

Abbie recoiled a step. "I-I can't do that."

Nigel looked exasperated. "Why not?"

"Because what's right is what's right," Abbie said quietly. "If there is a possibility that those vineyards were stolen, then you should want to return them, even if doing so will decrease your family fortunes." She frowned. "Honestly, I'm surprised George didn't restore them to their rightful owners." Her former husband might not have been very dashing. But he had been a good man, and Abbie had never known him to cheat or steal.

Nigel rolled his eyes. "As if grandfather told *George* about this. He was as witless as you are. He would've handed them straight back."

It was a small comfort, to know that George hadn't had a hand in this. "Then you admit that they rightfully should have been restored to Carlotta?"

"*Carlotta.*" Nigel's voice dripped with scorn. "Who gives a *damn* about Carlotta?"

Abbie flinched, more at his sentiment than his profanity. "How can you say such a thing?"

"Those vineyards would've been wasted on Carlotta! Even ignoring her whorish behavior after the end of her marriage, she had one purpose: to give my great uncle an heir. And she failed. She was nothing but a burden. To suggest that such a worthless creature somehow deserves an asset as lucrative as those vineyards is absurd!"

Abbie felt her throat constrict. This remark hit closer to home than Nigel had probably intended because she could empathize all too well with Carlotta's situation.

She, too, was a Dowager Lady Dulson.

One who had failed to produce an heir during her marriage.

One whom her family now saw as a burden.

But that didn't mean Nigel had the right of it.

"Carlotta de Noronha was not worthless!" Abbie said, her voice trembling. "Even if she never bore a single child, she had a beautiful spirit. It leaps off the page when you read her diary. She brought joy to everyone lucky enough to be near her, and her family treasured her for it. I know they did!"

Nigel's response was a roll of his eyes. "I've wasted enough of my time with this nonsense. You will give me that contract, or I will make you very sorry indeed."

"Well, I won't do it!"

He narrowed his eyes and stepped forward. "We can do this the easy way, or we can do it the hard way. Do not mistake me, Abigail. I am not *George*. I will not hesitate to tear your home apart, to pull every book off the shelf, to rip open every cushion, to smash every bottle in your pantry, if that is what it takes to find that contract. I suggest you hand it over!"

Abbie closed her fist around the object she'd been hiding beneath her skirts—one of her brother's pistols—then drew it from the holster and out of her pocket slit in one smooth motion. She pointed the gun at Nigel. "And I suggest you get off my property!"

He responded with a snort. "You probably don't even know how to use that thing."

"My brother was in the army. Do you really think he didn't teach me how to shoot? We used to practice every day when he was home from school." She cocked back the hammer, her motion smooth and easy. "I have my own little Queen Anne pistol, but I've always preferred these Wogdon and Barton dueling pistols. So much more accurate." She gave a dark laugh. "Truth be told, I prefer Hart's fowling piece. It was made by Joseph Manton himself. But I couldn't fit that beneath my dress."

Seeing that she knew what she was about, Nigel retreated

to the place where he'd tethered his horse. "This isn't over!" he snapped, yanking at the reins.

"Oh, but it is. This is my house. George left it to *me*. You have absolutely no right to come here without my permission. And you may consider my permission revoked!"

Nigel swung up onto his horse and gave an evil smile. "We'll see about that."

Abbie glowered after him as he galloped away. He might be the local lord.

But she had one last trump card in her hand, and by God, she was going to play it.

After instructing Brett and Mrs. Brownlee to bar Nigel from the house at all costs, she had her mare saddled and rode into Lymington. There was a militia stationed in town for the purpose of defending the coastline. She was the sister of a soldier who had given his life for king and country. That had to count for something.

The militia's commanding officer received her immediately. Major Oakley was more than sympathetic. It turned out he had been at school with Hart. It didn't matter a whit that Nigel was the local baron; Major Oakley would not countenance anyone harassing Captain Lord Hartlebury's little sister.

By dinnertime, two dozen soldiers were pitching tents in the meadow outside of Abbie's house, with the express instructions that it was to be guarded around the clock.

Although Abbie did not rest easy that first night, she did manage a few hours of sleep. And with each succeeding day in which Nigel did not come and try to ransack her house, the knot in the center of her chest slowly eased, until there were moments when she began to hope that Nigel had given up.

He hadn't.

He had something entirely different in mind.

CHAPTER 11

"I'm going to kill him," Gabe said.

"Gabe!" Abbie turned to gape at him. "You mustn't say such things."

He lifted his head enough to give her an incredulous look. "Surely you're not defending him?"

"Believe me, I'm not." She gave a bleak laugh. "Wait until you hear what he did next, and you'll understand the depth of my disdain for Nigel Davies. I absolutely want him to lose those vineyards, as I believe their rightful owner is Carlotta's family. But killing him is excessive."

"But, Abbie—"

She stroked a placating hand over his chest. "You have my permission to put the fear of God into him."

"I suppose that will have to serve," he grumbled. "I'm almost afraid to ask, but what is it that Nigel did next?"

"Well," Abbie said, settling in to continue her tale, "you see…"

THE LETTER ARRIVED one week after Abbie ran Nigel off her property.

She had assumed his line of attack would be directed at Carlotta. That he would try to discredit Abbie's copy of the marriage contract, and the statements Carlotta made in her diary. After all, who could trust the word of a whore—which was, sadly, a time-honored argument, and even more unfortunately, one that was likely to succeed. Or if that failed, Nigel would argue that the judge's ruling had become final regardless.

But Nigel didn't attack Carlotta.

He set out to ruin Abbie.

The letter was from a London barrister, notifying her that Nigel was contesting the terms of George's will. Specifically, he was challenging the clause granting Abbie the dower house and its contents, which, of course, included Carlotta's papers.

She had one week to come to London and file an answer.

She made her way hastily to town. The first three barristers she contacted about representing her turned her down. Nobody, it seemed, was eager to be seen publicly opposing a lord.

On her fourth attempt, she turned to Mr. Charles Vickery. Mr. Vickery's younger brother, Arnold, had served in the army alongside Hart, a connection she did not hesitate to press in her growing desperation. Fortunately, it worked, and Mr. Vickery agreed to represent her.

Abbie sat quietly while Mr. Vickery reviewed the lawsuit, as well as George's will. He was in his mid-forties and looked more like an army officer than a barrister, tall and fit with a barrel chest and just a touch of salt and pepper in his black hair. After what felt like an age, he removed his spectacles and slumped back in his chair, rubbing his forehead.

"Is it that bad?" Abbie asked.

"No. He has no case, none at all. Unless…" Mr. Vickery selected a particular document from the folio and spun it around for Abbie to read. "Your husband was nine and twenty when he died. Is there any evidence to support that he was not sound of mind?"

"None whatsoever."

"That is the only argument that might hold water—that he was not mentally capable, and you somehow coerced him into signing this. His will was properly executed, and the dower house was not part of the entail. See?" He indicated the relevant paragraph of another document, then leaned back, shaking his head. "That means your husband was free to dispose of it as he saw fit. There is no chance Lord Dulson will prevail in this."

His dismal expression was starkly at odds with his optimistic assessment of the case. "That sounds like good news," Abbie said hesitantly. "Is it not?"

"Look at this." Mr. Vickery selected another document and placed it before Abbie. "This details the discovery Lord Dulson has requested in connection with the case."

There were more than twenty lines of items. Nigel was requesting witness statements, expert testimony, and even a land survey. Abbie blanched, seeing that the fees associated with these activities came to more than three hundred pounds. "Am I expected to pay these costs?"

"Assuming the judge approves them, you are expected to pay half."

"That seems outrageously expensive!"

Mr. Vickery steepled his fingers, regarding her sadly from across his desk. "That is the point, my lady. And this is only the beginning. Mark my words, the discovery costs will continue to grow. And, although I am happy to charge you my lowest rate, I cannot afford to work without any pay, and it will take a significant amount of time for me to oversee all of this discovery."

Abbie swallowed. "I quite understand. I would never expect you to work for free. I appreciate you representing me at all."

He waved this off. "I've seen this before. As he has no case, his entire plan is to drag the case out for as long as possible and bury you in legal fees. When you can no longer afford to continue, he will win by default. It's a disgraceful tactic. It's also likely to be successful, particularly with the judge who's been assigned." He paused, studying Abbie for a moment. "Is there any reason his lordship would be so determined to recover the dower house?"

Abbie swallowed, hesitant to confess her most closely held secret to this man whom she had known for half an hour.

"I can see that there is. You must tell me the truth if I am to have a prayer of defending this case. As your barrister, I will hold anything you tell me in the strictest confidence. You have my word of honor."

Although she was loath to tell him, Abbie was running out of options. So she reached into her reticule and pulled out her copy of the marriage contract. "There is indeed. You see..."

Once she had finished, Mr. Vickery nodded gravely. "That would certainly explain Lord Dulson's determination to reclaim the dower house. With those vineyards providing such a significant portion of his income, he will surely stop at nothing to retain them."

"So it would seem." Abbie wrung her hands. "In terms of strategy, would it be wise to enter the marriage contract I found into evidence? In order to show the true motive behind this lawsuit?"

Mr. Vickery paused, considering. "To accuse a peer of fraud is a very serious matter. I'm not saying no. But we must be strategic in our timing. We need stronger evidence than what we currently have."

Abbie's shoulders fell a fraction. "I understand."

"I will begin by requesting a copy of the original court proceedings. That will shed some light on how your version of the marriage contract came to be invalidated." Mr. Vickery tapped his pen against the desk, thinking. "The other issue is that you are not the one who has been wrongfully deprived of these lands in Portugal. Under the terms of this marriage contract, they would have gone to Carlotta, but she apparently died without issue, and we do not have a copy of her will. As things stand right now, it looks almost like a victimless crime. It would be much more compelling were Carlotta's rightful heir to come forward and press the suit. Do you have any idea who that is?"

Abbie rubbed her temple. "I do not."

Mr. Vickery paused, studying her, then hesitatingly said, "You are in a very difficult position right now. I would be bereft in my duty as your barrister if I did not tell you that it is an option to settle. If you were to willingly sign the dower house over to Lord Dulson, you could preserve your nest egg, which is sufficient for you to rent a house. I may even be able to negotiate a more favorable agreement, as it appears his lordship is not truly after your home, but rather these papers."

Abbie shook her head. "What you're saying makes sense, but I could never live with myself if I handed the papers over to Nigel. It's the principle of the matter. Carlotta had a large family—three brothers and two sisters. I feel certain that an heir is out there, even if I don't know who he or she might be, nor how to get in contact with them. This is a life altering amount of property for the rightful owner. I could not sleep at night if I stood idly by."

She thought, but did not say, that it was more than that, more than a simple matter of right and wrong. That it was *personal*. She was not precisely sure what had happened sixty years ago, but all evidence suggested that George and Nigel's grandfather had conspired to cheat Carlotta, depriving her of her lawful property.

Abbie could relate. Oh, how she could relate! She had been deprived of her own dowry and browbeaten into marrying a man she didn't love. And just when she had gained a tiny modicum of dignity and control over her own life, here she was, once again on the cusp of disaster.

She was so, so sick of men thinking they could ride roughshod over her, simply because she was a woman. She could not bear the thought of letting Nigel cow her. She wasn't just doing this for herself, but also for Carlotta, her fellow dowager Lady Dulson, and the many women in this world who were dowager Lady Dulsons in spirit.

Mr. Vickery nodded. "Then we must set about finding the rightful heir. We know the location of the vineyards that were included in her dowry. We could send someone to Portugal to investigate. The only problem is that such an investigation would cost—"

"An astronomical sum, I'm sure." Abbie rubbed her temple, which was throbbing. "One I can ill afford."

"Do not fret, Lady Dulson. I will enter a response on your behalf and request a copy of that file. Reach out to some of your brother's friends in the army. Many of them spent years on the Peninsula. See if they know anyone near the Douro Valley to whom we could write. I'll ask my brother to do the same. It would reduce the cost of the investigation significantly if we could find someone who lives in the vicinity. That is where we must place our hopes. If we can but locate Carlotta's heirs in Portugal, our chances will improve significantly."

Abbie rose and shook his hand. "I'll reach out to Hart's friends immediately. Thank you, Mr. Vickery."

CHAPTER 12

Four weeks later, Abbie attended another hearing. It went every bit as badly as the previous three.

For an hour, she watched Mr. Vickery object to each item on Nigel's list of requested discovery as unnecessary to the case and inordinately expensive.

Each time, just as at the previous hearings, Judge Waring overruled him and approved the plaintiff's request.

Abbie did a quick tally in her head. Between the cost of the discovery approved today, Mr. Vickery's fees, and what she was being forced to pay for her London lodgings, she had just passed the one-thousand-pound mark.

That was a full quarter of the money George had left her, money that was meant to stay invested in stocks so it could produce an annuity for her to live on.

A quarter of her nest egg gone.

In one month.

Afterward, in the hallway, Mr. Vickery gave her what could only be described as a sympathetic grimace. "We must not despair. We still have every chance of success, if only the rightful heir can be found. Chin up, Lady Dulson."

He had another proceeding to attend, which suited Abbie, as she did not have to incur the expense of a hackney carriage in order to keep up appearances before her barrister. The lodging house where she had rented a room was in Soho, a neighborhood Abbie had selected both for its proximity to the Palace of Westminster, where the legal proceedings relating to Nigel's lawsuit took place, and its affordability compared to its neighbor, Mayfair. The weather was not particularly fine, but it wasn't a downpour, and she was only a mile away from her lodgings. She could manage the walk.

She hadn't gone a quarter mile when a black lacquered carriage pulled to the curb next to her. Much to her astonishment, two footmen hopped down from the back of the conveyance, seized her by the arms, and shoved her into the carriage.

"Unhand me!" she shrieked as the door slammed shut and the carriage began moving. "Somebody help—"

"Oh, do shut up."

Abbie froze upon hearing a voice that was as familiar as it was unwelcome. She glanced across the carriage, and her suspicions were confirmed.

"Nigel, this is an outrage! What on earth are you doing?"

"Negotiating. Don't you think it's time to put this silly misunderstanding behind us?"

She lifted her chin. "This is entirely inappropriate. Considering you are suing me, I do not wish to speak to you without my barrister present."

"Yes, well, you may convey my offer to your barrister."

She cut her eyes to him warily. "What offer?"

Nigel's smile reminded her of a cat toying with its prey. "I think you saw today that this proceeding is not going to go well for you."

Abbie stiffened but said nothing.

"George left you four thousand pounds in your annuity," Nigel continued. "Which produces enough income for you to live on. But not if you have to spend down the principle." Nigel leaned forward, enunciating his words so she could not fail to escape their meaning. "You will be destitute. In a year, perhaps two, you will have *nothing*. Unless…"

"I will not give you what you want," Abbie snapped. "You have stolen someone's legacy. And what is most ghastly, you know it, yet you will do nothing to make things right. Some of us have principles."

"Principles." Nigel made a sound of mock admiration. "A wonderful thing, to be sure. But *principles*, Abigail, will not put a roof over your head nor food on your table. I wonder what you will have to do to survive once they are the only thing you have left. Something, I fear, that violates those cherished principles."

Abbie's spine stiffened. She knew exactly what Nigel was implying, that once she had lost everything else, a woman had only one thing she could sell. How on earth had her life been reduced to this? She was the daughter of an earl, and she had married a peer.

And yet, here she was, friendless and alone, and on the brink of destitution.

She bit her lip to stop it from quivering. She would not rise to Nigel's bait, nor would she give in to despair. "You said you had a proposal for me. Tell me this instant, or I am getting out of this carriage."

"It has occurred to me that it is time to bring you back into the fold." Nigel's eyes strayed down and came to linger flagrantly, lasciviously, on Abbie's bosom. "Marry me, return the dower house—and its full contents—to the Dulson estate, and let's forget about this whole sordid business."

"You are the *last* man I would *ever* marry!" Abbie spat. She rapped on the roof of the carriage. "Stop! Let me out!"

"My lord?" the coachman called from his place on the box.

"It's all right, John," Nigel said with a wave of his hand. "Our conversation has concluded."

The carriage pulled to the curb. Abbie worked the latch with hands that shook and wrenched the door open, not bothering to wait for the footmen. She stumbled out onto the pavement in her haste to escape.

"Think about what I have said," Nigel called, leaning forward so he could glare at her from inside the carriage.

Abbie made a slashing motion. "I have already given you my answer."

"I will give you one week to properly consider it. If you do not accept it in that time, you may consider it withdrawn." Nigel's eyes were hard as he added, "And you will face the consequences of your decision alone."

A footman closed the door and the carriage pulled away, leaving Abbie standing on the pavement as a light drizzle fell, her chest heaving as if she'd run all the way from the Palace of Westminster.

She glanced around. Nigel had deposited her just outside of Green Park.

Green Park seemed as good a place as any to contemplate her impending penury. The dreary weather meant that the park wasn't crowded. And so, she spent the next hour wandering listlessly down the graveled paths, turning her problems over and over in her head. Her options were few, and each more unappealing than the last.

Uncle Edmond was the only family she had left. She doubted he would take her in, but if he did, the constant remarks about how she was a drain upon the family's resources would make her life a misery.

She could keep up the legal fight, but for how long? At the rate expenses were currently accumulating, her nest egg would be gone before the year was out. And once her money was gone, she would have to make some hard choices. Perhaps she could find work as a governess, or as a paid companion, rather than having to become some man's mistress. Although honestly, Abbie had seen enough of the world to know that a young, somewhat pretty woman in those positions was regarded as sexually available by whatever men were part of the household. For many women, the positions of courtesan and governess had a surprising degree of overlap in job duties. The best-case scenario would be if she could find a rich dowager who lived on her own, but she could think of no such friend or acquaintance who might want a companion.

The only other possibility was finding a rich man to marry.

Abbie laughed blackly at that absurd idea. She might have once had enough youthful charm to catch a man's eye. But that felt like a lifetime ago. Now she felt about as lively as a funeral. The notion that she could snare a rich man felt preposterous enough, but to do so in the space of one week?

Impossible.

And that left... Nigel.

Perhaps he wouldn't be such a bad husband. She hadn't wanted to marry George, but in many ways, he had been a good husband. He hadn't understood her a whit, but George had tried. He had been kind to her, in a clumsy sort of way.

But Nigel was not George. She wondered if he would beat her. As her husband, he would be within his rights to do so, and she had no living male relatives who would object on her behalf.

Gabe would object. She had read about his situation in the papers and knew that he had inherited his great-uncle's title. Unfortunately, he had also inherited his great-uncle's debts, meaning there was no possibility he could marry her.

But surely he would be coming back to England now that he had inherited. And his presence on English soil afforded Abbie some level of protection. He would call Nigel out or threaten to beat the living daylights out of him if he laid a hand upon Abbie. She knew that he would.

Yes, with Gabe back on English soil, marriage to Nigel would be… not tolerable.

But perhaps survivable.

And so Abbie found herself wandering listlessly through Green Park, trying to resign herself to her status as the once and future Lady Dulson when a feminine voice interrupted her ruminations. "What's wrong, dear?"

The voice belonged to a woman of about sixty years with high cheekbones and an angular face whose harshness was offset by the warmth of her brown eyes. Abbie soon learned that she was Katherine Lockley, the Countess of Wyndham. Lady Wyndham possessed a quality that was difficult to describe. Although she was not tall, she managed to be imposing, with a self-assured set to her shoulders and an ornate mahogany walking stick that Abbie suspected she would not hesitate to use as a bludgeon should the situation require it. But somehow Abbie knew at once that she had encountered someone who cared, someone who would listen.

So Abbie spent the next hour sitting on a bench in Green Park with Lady Wyndham, pouring out her troubles. It felt good to have someone in whom she could confide, even if Lady Wyndham could not materially change Abbie's situation.

Once Abbie came to the end of her sad tale, she pressed Lady Wyndham's hand. "Thank you so much for listening to me."

"Of course, dear." Lady Wyndham patted Abbie's hand three times, then stood. "Now, come on."

"Come on?" Abbie asked, surprised. "Where are we going?"

"Why, to Matron Manor, of course!"

"Matron Manor?" Abbie tilted her head at the odd name. "Where is Matron Manor?"

"It's in Mayfair. But the more pertinent question is not *where* Matron Manor is, but rather *what* it is."

"All right," Abbie said, confused. "What is Matron Manor?"

Lady Wyndham rapped her cane against the gravel path. "It is the headquarters of my Wicked Widows' League! And your new home, for as long as you need it. Come!"

CHAPTER 13

"The Wicked Widows' League?" Gabe asked. He had propped a few pillows up against the headboard, and they were reclining against them while Abbie told him her story. "Dare I to ask what the Wicked Widows' League is?"

"You might call it a club."

Gabe waited for her to elaborate. She did not. "But why *wicked* widows? What sort of wickedness do they get up to?" He chuckled nervously. "They don't go around poisoning people, do they?"

Abbie rolled her eyes. "Nothing of the sort. They merely want to live life on their own terms. They hold property in their own names and manage their own financial affairs. They also take lovers, if they want one and the gentleman is agreeable." She poked him in the arm. "You know, the sort of behavior men engage in every day without being called a harlot."

Gabe inclined his head, conceding the point. He was hardly in a position to cast any stones. "Well, I can't argue against that. But why did they form a club?"

"It is fortunate for me that they did because, without the club, they would not own Matron Manor, where I am presently staying free of charge while Nigel pursues his case."

Thank God. The thought of Abbie being forced to marry Nigel was intolerable. Of course, the notion of her marrying *any* other man made his chest twist up in knots. But the possibility of her finding herself bound to a man who would be cruel to her made him want to break things, starting with the nose of this imaginary future husband.

Gabe cleared his throat. "They'll let you stay there indefinitely, then?"

"Lady Wyndham has said as much, even though I am not able to pay the club's usual dues."

Gabe let his head loll back against the pillows, his neck and shoulders untensing. "Thank God. That means you can forget all this nonsense about having to marry Nigel." He waited a few beats for Abbie to agree with him, but she remained stubbornly silent. He peered up at her. "Can't you, Abbie?"

She squeezed her eyes shut. "I just don't know."

Gabe sat up, taking her hands in his. She tried to avoid his eye, but he was having none of it. "Abbie, look at me." He needed her full attention. This was *important.*

When she reluctantly cut her eyes to his, he said, "How can you even consider marrying Nigel when you have a viable alternative?"

"But is it viable?" Abbie asked, her voice rising in pitch. "I have known these women for all of four days. Do not mistake me—they have been wonderful. It's not merely that they have allowed me to stay at Matron Manor. They have helped me and supported me in so many ways. They contrived to get me an invitation to Lady Styring's ball on the off chance that I could catch the eye of some rich man."

Gabe stiffened. He knew damn well he had no right to

complain. But the thought of Abbie being swept off her feet at a ball by some sod lucky enough to have inherited a fortune along with his title made the feral beast inside of him snarl.

He struggled to keep his voice even. "And did you?"

Abbie laughed as if this was an absurd question. Gabe frowned. Did she truly not understand how beautiful she was? That she was desirable and wonderful in every possible way?

Abbie was speaking, so he made an effort to attend. "Of course, I didn't. But while I was there, I overheard Cordelia Fitzherbert—you might remember her, she's the daughter of one of Uncle Edmond's friends. She was always dangling after Hart."

Gabe groaned. If it was the girl he was thinking of, she had always looked at him like something unpleasant she had just stepped in. "I think so. Blonde hair, impressive sneer?"

"The very one. Well, she was at the punch table with her friends and didn't realize I was standing behind her. She mocked my gown for being last season's fashion, referred to me as Lady *Dull*-son, and said, 'Can you believe that she was once considered to be vivacious?'"

Gabe scowled, disliking Cordelia Fitzherbert ten times more for making Abbie feel sad than for anything she'd ever done to him. "I hope you spilled punch on her."

"The Wicked Widows did her one better. You see, when Cordelia made the remark, I was standing between Lady Sylvan and Lady Covington, who are both on the Wicked Widows' Council—"

Gabe ran a hand over his face. "Dear God, they have a council."

"—and just before Cordelia was to dance with the Earl of Marbury, Lady Sylvan sneaked up behind her and slipped a piece of ice down the back of her dress."

That startled a grin out of him. "Did she truly?"

"She most certainly did! She broke it off one of the ice sculptures. She said it was quite a big piece, the size of her palm. Well, Cordelia shrieked and began flailing her arms, trying to get it out. Absolutely everyone was staring at her. But, of course, no one knew what had happened, or why she was behaving so strangely. She had to beat a hasty retreat to the ladies' retiring room and missed her dance with Lord Marbury in the process. His lordship did not seem overly disappointed. She looked a bit… unhinged."

Gabe chuckled. "I've changed my mind. I like these Wicked Widows."

"And," Abbie said, poking him in the chest, "it was the Wicked Widows who let me know about the bachelor auction and encouraged me to enter." Gabe enjoyed the becoming blush that spread across her cheeks. "I argued against it at first, but when I saw your name on the list of prospective bachelors, I surrendered with remarkable alacrity."

Gabe started. "But wait—Abbie, you can't afford to give me a thousand pounds! You're already in financial straits thanks to Nigel, and—"

She waved this off. "I'm not worried about that. I know you'll pay me back once you've found some rich heiress." She kept her voice light as she discussed his future bride, but she cut her gaze to the mattress and based on the tightness that came into her eyes, Gabe fancied the topic was no easier for her than it was for him.

She continued with forced brightness, "Then there's the fact that if I'm forced to marry Nigel, whatever money is left in my estate will go to him. I would quite prefer for you to have it."

Gabe groaned. "Abbie, you can't marry Nigel. You absolutely can't. As his wife, he would have complete control over you. He could lock you away. He could beat you. He could—"

"I know, Gabe. Believe me, I know. But my only other option is to rely upon the charity of the Wicked Widows. And, as wonderful as they are, I haven't even known them a full week! Will they still be so eager to support me a year from now? Ten years from now?" Her voice had grown shrill, and Gabe could tell she had been turning these thoughts over in her head for days.

"How will I feel," Abbie continued, "imposing upon them to that degree? Marriage to Nigel would be intolerable. But the only alternative has so many unknowns. It's easy to imagine that the widows could change their minds, and I could find myself in even worse circumstances." She rubbed her temple. "I go back and forth between the Widows and Nigel, changing my mind, a dozen times a day. I don't know what I'm going to do. I don't seem to have any good choices before me." She gave a bitter laugh. "I keep hoping for a miracle, that Carlotta's heir will magically appear. And maybe they will. But as of right now, I have no idea who they might be."

"Speaking of Carlotta's heir"—Gabe held a hand up at Abbie's startled look—"I don't want to get your hopes up. It will probably come to nothing. But I know someone with the last name of de Noronha from my time in Portugal."

Abbie, who had been avoiding his gaze before, sat up, seizing his hand. "Who?"

"An officer I served with. He was with one of the Portuguese Infantry Divisions, and we were on campaign together for a time. Good chap. Captain Santiago de Noronha."

Abbie bit her lip, despair and hope warring in her eyes. "Do you think he might be a relation of Carlotta's?"

Gabe grimaced, wishing he could give her a reason to

hope. "I have no idea. I'm not sure how common of a last name de Noronha is. But I do know that his family owns a vineyard. When we would dine together, he could tell you everything about the wine, just from tasting it. It was remarkable." He held up a hand. "But I don't want you to read too much into that. Owning a vineyard is not so uncommon in Portugal. In any case, I wrote to him upon receiving your letter. Then three days later, I received the news that my great-uncle had died and found myself on a ship back to England. If he responds, the letter will probably go to Malta, and we'll have to wait an extra month for it to be forwarded if it's forwarded at all."

"I see." Abbie fidgeted with the fringe on the counterpane. "I will try to temper my expectations." Suddenly she looked up at him, her eyes sincere. "Thank you for writing to him, regardless of whether anything comes of it. For helping me."

He reached out, tucking a curl that honestly was not wayward behind her ear. Any excuse to touch her. "You're welcome."

He was pleased when she leaned into his hand. He trailed his fingers down the side of her neck and was rewarded with a shiver. By the time he traced her finely sculpted collarbone, a becoming blush had flooded her cheeks.

"Gabe," she burst out, "could I ask you a question?"

"Of course." He continued his ministrations, stroking across her shoulder and down her arm.

"It's probably a stupid question," she muttered, ducking her chin.

He was reminded that, widow or no, there remained a gulf of experience separating them. He made sure his face was solemn as he replied, "There are no stupid questions."

She couldn't meet his eye as she asked, "Is it possible for a man to make love with a woman more than once in a single night?"

Gabe couldn't help it.

He smiled.

"Why, yes, Abbie," he said, dipping his hand beneath the satin counterpane she had tucked up under her arms and teasing her already-hard nipples, "it is absolutely possible." He used his other hand to stroke his chin as if deep in thought. "Perhaps it would be best if I were to demonstrate."

As his lips descended upon hers, she was smiling, too.

CHAPTER 14

*O*ne could be forgiven for expecting that, in the moment Gabe was about to make love to the woman he'd pined after for the last nine years, his feelings would be somewhere along the continuum between excitement and elation.

And he did feel those things. But his joy was tempered by the knowledge that this would be his one and only night with Abbie.

She grabbed his arms, trying to push him back onto the bed, but he stopped her. "Wait," he said, breathing hard. They had so little time together, so he wanted to do something truly special for her.

To give her the memory of a lifetime.

He seated her upon the edge of the bed but didn't join her there. She must've felt exposed by the position because she wrapped the sheet around her body.

Gabe crossed the room in three steps and seized a cheval mirror. He brought it over to the bed, placing it directly before her.

"Gabe?" she asked uncertainly.

He knelt behind her on the bed and leaned forward to whisper seductively in her ear. "I want you to have an unimpeded view. You're going to remember this moment forever. Tonight, I'm going to worship you like the goddess you are, in the way that you deserve." He pressed a kiss to her ear, then added, "And you're going to watch me do it."

She seemed shy about looking at herself, so he gently took her chin in his hand and raised it. She finally met his gaze in the mirror, her eyes guarded. "Look at yourself, Abbie," he murmured. He traced his hands up her arms, across the delicate arch of her collarbone, then up the delicate skin of her neck. He caught sight of himself in the mirror, and the admiration was plain upon his own face. *Good. Let her see herself through my eyes.*

The sheet slipped to her waist, and Gabe was pleased that she made no move to catch it. "Look at how beautiful you are. How perfect." He cupped her breasts in his hands, savoring their sweet weight, and could not suppress a groan. He pressed his body against the delicious softness of her bottom, and his swollen cock pulsed, begging for some attention. "Do you feel what you do to me? How much I want you?"

Abbie's gaze was now transfixed upon the mirror, her initial shyness having dissolved into thin air. "Yes," she breathed.

He kissed his way down her neck, reaching around to suckle first one ripe breast, then the other. He lingered, teasing her there until her breath was coming in pants and her hips began to squirm from side to side, searching for some friction. That was his cue to delve lower with his hand, beneath the sheets and between her legs. She cried out at first contact and tried to lie back upon the bed, but he held her upright.

"Stay right there." He unwrapped her fully, then came

around to stand in front of her. He kissed her deeply, then breathed in her ear, "You bring me to my knees."

He dropped down before her, ready and eager to worship her. The bed was high, and kneeling, he was at the perfect height, his face level with her most intimate parts. He spread her petal-soft thighs and groaned at the sight of her, all pink and perfect and slick, just for him. The flush on her creamy skin betrayed her self-consciousness, but when he started kissing his way up the inside of her thigh, she didn't tell him to stop.

He breathed deeply, wanting to remember every second of this, from the way she looked in the candlelight to the sweet scent of her. He pressed his lips against her core, tenderly, reverently.

But Abbie was having none of it. She was far enough gone that she immediately threaded her fingers through his hair and guided his mouth directly to that sweet little spot hidden within her folds.

He chuckled against her petal-soft skin. "All right, minx, I'll give you what you want. On one condition." He tilted his head toward the mirror. "You have to watch."

Abbie nodded, her eyes shiny. And then Gabe parted the sweet curls at the juncture of her thighs and delved in with his tongue. He didn't tease her but immediately experimented with light flicks versus circles versus massaging her with the flat of his tongue to see what best pleased her. Receiving the most encouraging response when he started light suction, he continued with that, gradually ratcheting up the intensity until Abbie's legs started to tremble and she screamed his name.

He stood, and she tried to pull him to her. But Gabe resisted, stepping back to slip on a fresh condom before climbing up behind her on the bed. He kissed her neck, reaching around to caress her breasts as he urged her up onto her knees. "I like to watch, too," he murmured huskily in her ear.

"Gabe?" she asked uncertainly as he guided his straining cock toward her opening. "Can we really…?"

"We can," he said, his voice tight. He reached up to the headboard and snagged a couple of pillows, which he placed beneath Abbie's knees to boost her up. *Much better.* Now he had the angle he needed…

Abbie gasped as his cock glided in and instinctively spread her thighs wider. Gabe groaned at the incandescent pleasure of her warm tightness, still slick from the pleasure he'd given her just moments before. He pressed kisses into her neck as he slowly pressed forward until he was fully seated.

Meeting her eyes in the mirror, he began to thrust. It was unbearably erotic, looking her in the eye as he made love to her. He could see his own expression, could see his heart laid bare upon his face. But that was all right, because Abbie looked much the same way. All the while, he made good use of his hands, stroking up her arms, teasing her nipples until her hips began to buck, and then stroking down over her downy stomach to once again settle between her legs.

He then proceeded to show her the real advantage of this position: the easy access it granted to that little pearl that was the center of her pleasure. She wasn't too sensitive if the way she grabbed his wrist to hold his hand in place was any indication. Gabe was teetering on the edge of his own climax, and the erotic sight that greeted him in the mirror, of Abbie's eyes, glassy with pleasure, did nothing to help him hold back. But his desire to give her pleasure was even stronger than his need to come, and although he would never know how he did it, he managed to suppress his own peak until Abbie began to shake in his arms.

Then he thrust with abandon, still working her sweet

rosebud with fingers slick with her honey, and he cried out against her neck as the pleasure overwhelmed him.

Abbie fell limp as a ragdoll. Gabe was fairly sure he was the only thing holding her up. That was all right. He drew her gently to the head of the bed, settled her in his arms, and pulled the covers up over them.

She seemed drowsily content, and he thought she might fall asleep, but she surprised him by whispering, "This might be the happiest I've ever been. I just wish I was a great heiress, so I could be the one who gets to marry you."

Gabe froze, unsure what to say. Of course, he wanted the same thing. His dreams of being with Abbie were what had sustained him through nine years on campaign.

But those had been dreams. Nothing more. Now that he was contemplating it, the thought of actually marrying Abbie was enough to make him break out in hives. That wouldn't be merely breaking his vow to Hart. It would be *flaunting* it. The thought of his best friend scowling down at him from heaven was enough to make any man feel a twinge of guilt.

And besides—he was the man his own family hadn't even wanted. He'd spent his entire life knowing that he was good for one thing, and one thing only: cannon fodder. The suggestion that *he* was worthy of *Abbie*…

It was ludicrous, is what it was. Ludicrous and incomprehensible.

She was awaiting his response, so he forced a weak chuckle. "I'm sure you could do better than the likes of me."

He'd hoped she would let it go, but she rolled onto her stomach, propping a hand beneath her chin. Those aquamarine eyes studied him, and he had to suppress the instinct to squirm. "You don't really think that. Do you?"

He tried to wave it off. "Of course not. I was only jesting."

"I'm not sure I believe that." She tilted her head to the

side. "Is this because of the promise Hart forced you to make?"

He cleared his throat. "Come on, Abbie. Everyone knows I'm a scoundrel."

"I don't. A mere scoundrel would not have sent me such feeling letters."

He stared at the ceiling, unable to meet her eye. "Look, tonight has been enjoyable. More than enjoyable. Let's not ruin it."

"Is that what I would be doing by telling you that I love you? Ruining it?"

Gabe's good intentions of keeping his eyes fixed upon the plasterwork above him flew out the window. He searched Abbie's face, trying to figure out if she meant those words, or if her question had been hypothetical. Part of him wanted to ask, and part of him was afraid of the answer. Not that he had much choice in the matter, as his tongue suddenly felt thick and leaden in his mouth.

Fortunately—or unfortunately, he couldn't decide which it was—Abbie anticipated the question he couldn't manage to form. "Because I do love you, Gabe. I always have. But recently, I've become surer than ever that you're the man I want to spend my life with."

"Because I inherited my great-uncle's title," Gabe blurted.

Abbie bit her lip. "I hope you don't really believe that. I don't give a fig about your title. I would want to marry you just as much if you were still a simple army lieutenant." She took his hand and brushed her thumb across the back of his knuckles. "And the reason I want to marry you is because of your letters. They showed me what kind of man you really are."

Gabe grunted and looked away. Which he knew was not the right response.

But honestly, what was he supposed to say? That he loved her, too? He did, but what did it matter? He was going to have to marry someone else regardless of how they felt about each other.

If he had any shred of decency, he would tell Abbie that he didn't feel the same way. It might be a lie, but in the end, it would be kinder to make a clean break. She would hate him, but if it enabled her to move on and eventually find happiness with another man, a man who could marry her, wouldn't that be better than for her to waste years longing for something neither of them could ever have?

But when she peered up at him, her eyes filled with uncertainty, and asked, "Do you love me, too, Gabe?" he couldn't do it, couldn't bear to be quite so cruel.

So he looked away and muttered, "I don't want to hurt you, Abbie."

At least that was true. When he chanced a glance at Abbie to see if he'd succeeded in dissuading her, he found that she had turned to face the wall.

Guilt rose like bile in his throat. Maybe it had been a mistake to deny that he loved her.

Although… God, if he couldn't bear to hurt her now, in this small way, how would he feel knowing he had ruined her life by giving her hope when there was none?

He didn't know what the hell to say, what the right thing was. He lay there, his brain scrambling for anything he could say to make the situation better and coming up blank.

Abbie solved his dilemma for him. "I'm tired," she announced, reaching for the bedside lamp with fumbling fingers. "And I have another legal hearing first thing in the morning. Let's get some rest."

Gabe grunted his assent, but sleep did not come easily. He lay for hours, staring at the ceiling in the shadowy moonlight.

Abbie might be mere inches away. But she felt as far away as she'd been the last nine years.

CHAPTER 15

The following morning, beneath the brave face Abbie put on for Gabe's benefit, her emotions were a jumbled mess, veering from despondency to acceptance to humiliation, all within a span of two minutes.

She wasn't sorry she had told him that she loved him. Hart's death had taught her that life was too often short. However many years she had left, she wanted to live them bravely, and she wasn't unwilling to take a risk by confessing her feelings to Gabe.

Still, was there anything more humiliating than telling a man you loved him and him not saying it back? A part of Abbie was glad that, after tossing and turning for hours, they overslept the following morning, so that she had to hurriedly dress for today's hearing. As much as she would've liked to make love to him one final time, she wasn't sure that she could go through with it—at least, not without bursting into tears.

She sneaked a sideways peek at Gabe as they made their way toward the hearing room. He had insisted upon accompanying her to Westminster Hall, muttering that if there was any chance she was going to accept Nigel's proposal, he was going to make it clear that there would be *consequences* if her new husband did not treat her well.

They had just found a bit of space to wait outside the hearing room when a flurry of murmurs went up from the far end of the hallway. Abbie joined those who surrounded her in craning her neck, trying to see the cause of the commotion.

Gabe suddenly broke out into a grin. "Well, I'll be damned!"

Abbie wasn't tall enough to see over the crowd. "What is it, Gabe?"

"Not what. *Who.*" He looked down at her, and his grin was so bright, he was practically glowing. "It appears your prayers have been answered."

Abbie tilted her head. Her prayers? What on earth did Gabe mean by that? Hadn't he been the one to dash her every hope the night before?

"De Noronha!" Gabe called, waving a hand overhead. "Over here!"

Suddenly it was hard to breathe. Had Abbie misheard? Had the stress finally gotten to her, causing her mind to break? Because it sounded like Gabe had said... like he had just said...

The man who came striding down the hall was an officer, and at first glance, his dark blue coat trimmed with gold braid brought to mind the Royal Navy. But then Abbie noticed the shako he carried under his arm, the bright red sash at his waist, and the white tassels bouncing against his hip, all of which marked him as an officer of the Portuguese army.

He was younger than Gabe, perhaps around Abbie's age, and handsome, with silky black hair and fine dark eyes. His figure was trim and he was of medium height, but he had impeccable posture and an air of command that drew every eye in the crowded hallway.

"I can't believe you're here!" Gabe cried, clasping the man's hand and pumping it. "Bloody hell!"

A few heads jerked in Gabe's direction at this profanity. "Sorry," Gabe called in response to the disapproving looks. "Just left the army. Still adjusting to polite society."

He turned back to the man in uniform. "I've never been so glad to see you."

His friend replied in English seasoned with a musical accent. "Not half as glad as I was to see you during the Battle of Vitoria, I daresay."

Gabe ducked his head, leading Abbie to wonder what had him feeling so embarrassed. He was already turning to her. "Allow me to present my good friend and comrade-in-arms, Captain Santiago de Noronha of the Second Portuguese Infantry Division."

"Oh, no!" Captain de Noronha seized Abbie's hand and gave her a seductive smile. "When a man meets such a beautiful woman, he wishes to hear his own name upon her lips." He pressed a lingering kiss upon the back of Abbie's glove, and when he lifted his head, his eyes simmered. "You, *minha linda*, must call me Tiago."

"That's enough of *that*," Gabe said grumpily, placing a hand on his friend's shoulder and shoving him to the side. He claimed Abbie's hand and put it pointedly on his arm, shooting a scowl at the friend he had so recently been glad to see.

Tiago laughed, tugging his coat back into place. "Goodness, Davenport. From the way you're carrying on, one would think this was your Abigail."

Abbie's mouth fell open. *His* Abigail? Since when was she *his* Abigail?

Gabe had some explaining to do. She looked up and found him cringing.

Tiago glanced back and forth between the two of them, and his face cracked into a broad smile. "You are! You are his Abbie! Oh, this is better than I could have hoped—already he has claimed his happiness!" He stood erect, abruptly proper, and bowed again, this time stopping the requisite two inches above Abbie's hand. "In that case, I will behave myself, but you still must call me Tiago."

"Thank you, Tiago. And you are correct. I am Abigail Davies." She glanced at Gabe, who had his mouth resolutely clamped shut. She turned back to Tiago. "May I ask what you meant when you said that I was *his* Abigail?"

Tiago recoiled, then turned to glare at Gabe. "Do you mean to tell me you have not already proposed? What on earth are you waiting for? Given what you have told me about your beloved Abigail, I would have expected you to fly to her side, to waste not a single second in—"

"It's complicated," Gabe ground out.

Abbie was reeling. Since when was she Gabe's *beloved* Abigail? Why, just last night he had denied having feelings for her. And while a little voice inside her head kept asking *but what if he's lying*, each time it piped up she had brutally quashed it. The more rational part of her brain knew that this was wistful thinking, nothing more.

And yet… If what Tiago was saying was true, if she wasn't misunderstanding… Oh, what if she *was* misunderstanding? What if she was beloved in the way of a little sister?

Tiago had an outraged expression on his handsome face. "Complicated?" He gestured to Abbie. "What is complicated about marrying the woman you love?"

Abbie all but choked on her own tongue. *That* didn't leave much room for misinterpretation.

She rounded on Gabe, hands upon her hips. "The woman you love, hmm? Care to explain, Gabe?"

Gabe said nothing, so she turned back to the captain. "Tiago, what exactly has Gabe told you about me?"

A mischievous glint came into Tiago's brown eyes. "It was only when he was deep into his cups that he would talk about you. But then he would tell us of a girl, a girl unparalleled in beauty, and in kindness—"

"De Noronha," Gabe said sharply.

"Oh, how he lived for your letters!" Tiago continued, unrepentant. "Every time he would receive one, he would disappear into his tent for *hours*—"

Gabe's cheeks had a distinct pink tinge beneath his golden tan. "That's enough."

"But oh, the agony!" Tiago pressed a hand to his heart. "Because Abigail, *his* Abigail, was wed to another!"

"I think you've embarrassed me sufficiently," Gabe said. "You can stop now."

"But then," Tiago continued, raising a finger in triumph, "her husband died! There was a chance, a chance for him to be with his beloved at long last! So you can imagine my surprise, to find the two of you here together and to learn that he has not proposed."

"Remind me again why we're friends," Gabe muttered.

Tiago turned to Gabe. "Is it that nonsense about feeling unworthy of her?" He fixed his eyes upon Abbie. "Because he is worthy, *minha linda*. Believe me, he is worthy."

"I am well aware of it," Abbie concurred.

"See!" Tiago reached behind Gabe and gave him an encouraging push forward. "She is receptive to your suit! Why do you not—"

"Santiago?" came a more heavily accented voice from just behind them.

Tiago snapped to attention. "*Avô.*" He drew an elderly

man into their circle. The man was half a head shorter than Tiago and had a full head of salt-and-pepper hair and a neatly groomed mustache. Although he had to be in his eighties, his posture remained upright, and he carried himself with grave dignity.

To Gabe and Abbie, Tiago said, "This is my grandfather, Rodrigo de Noronha." He continued in Portuguese, "Grandfather, allow me to present my friends. This is Lieutenant Davenport—"

"*Davenport?*" Mr. de Noronha's wide eyes flew to Tiago's face, and then to Gabe's. "Do you mean, *the* Lieutenant Davenport?"

"The very one," Tiago replied.

"The Lieutenant Davenport who fought with you at Vitoria?"

"Yes, Grandfather."

Tiago's grandfather stood frozen for a breath, staring at Gabe intently.

Then, all at once, he surged forward, catching Gabe in a bear hug, right in the middle of the hallway of Westminster Hall in front of several dozen shocked witnesses.

"Thank you," he said into Gabe's cravat. "Thank you, on behalf of the entire de Noronha family, and from the bottom of my heart."

Gabe was stuck, obviously uncomfortable, but unable to extract himself without manhandling an eighty-year-old man. "Oh, er, it was nothing, sir," he said in Portuguese, trying to gently loosen Mr. de Noronha's grip on his jacket.

"Nothing!" Mr. de Noronha relaxed just enough to stare up at Gabe incredulously. "I would not call saving the life of my only surviving grandson nothing!"

"It's—it's quite all right," Gabe muttered.

"Seven grandsons, I once had!" Mr. de Noronha continued, oblivious to Gabe's discomfort. "Seven! All of them proudly volunteered to protect their country. One by one, they were cut down by the madman Bonaparte, until my Tiago was the only one left. Then I come to find out that he would have suffered the same fate, were it not for you! You are the reason my family's name will continue!" He squeezed Gabe even tighter. "Ever since we learned what you did for our Tiago, we have prayed for you. Yes, every single day, the entire de Noronha family prays for our heavenly Father to bless and watch over our dear friend Lieutenant Davenport."

"I'm sure I need it," Gabe said. "Thank you."

"Come, *Avô*," Tiago said, smoothly extracting his grandfather from around Gabe's waist. "I know you are overjoyed to meet Lieutenant Davenport. But we must not embarrass him. You know how stilted the English are about these things."

"Ah, of course," Mr. de Noronha said, straightening his jacket. "My apologies, Lieutenant."

"Not at all, sir," Gabe hastened to say.

Tiago gestured to Abbie. "You will also want to meet Abigail Davies. Like Carlotta, she is a dowager Lady Dulson. She is the one who found your sister's diary, as well as the marriage contract, in the dower house."

Your sister's diary. The hope that had been budding in her chest ever since Tiago came striding down the hall burst into bloom. "Mr. de Noronha," Abbie said in Portuguese, "what a pleasure. I can hardly believe my ears. Are you truly Carlotta's brother?"

"I am," Mr. de Noronha said. He started to reach for Abbie's hands but stopped himself with a chuckle. "I know it is not the done thing here. But we are almost as grateful to you as we are to Lieutenant Davenport there."

It was Abbie who took his hand, pressing it in both of hers. "Not half so grateful as I am to see you."

His eyes were bright as he laughed. "It is not possible. You see, the lands my father granted to Carlotta were right in the heart of the de Noronha vineyard. He intended that her children would always have ties to our lands, and to our family. That they would not become strangers to us." He shook his head. "Those lands were not given lightly. Nothing is more important to us than family, you see. So to have them stolen from us by this Baron Dulson, who was so callous toward my sister, and who had no interest in being a part of our family, has been like a wound upon my heart for all these years."

"Oh, this is too wonderful," Abbie said. "I knew there had to be a reason I was holding out."

Mr. de Noronha tilted his head to the side. "Holding out? What do you mean, holding out?"

She quickly filled them in on Nigel's scheme to force her to give up her copy of the marriage contract. Both Tiago and his grandfather were outraged on her behalf.

"Please, do not distress yourself," Abbie begged. "For the first time in so long, I believe that everything will be all right. Now that you are here, my hopes are rekindled."

Just then, Mr. Vickery approached. "Ah, Lady Dulson, there you are." He stopped short, noticing her companions.

"Mr. Vickery, you will not believe the good news!" Abbie quickly introduced Gabe, Tiago, and Mr. de Noronha, and explained how they had come to be there.

Mr. Vickery's body sagged. "Thank God. My lady, given this change in circumstances, I think the time has come to reveal the true reason Nigel is pursuing this suit against you. Would you agree?"

"I would," Abbie said.

"Good," Mr. Vickery said. "Gentlemen, if you would be so kind as to accompany me, I believe we are next on Judge Waring's docket."

No sooner had they queued up outside the door than it swung open.

And out strode the Duke of Wellington.

Gabe and Tiago both snapped to attention at the sight of their former battlefield commander. The duke jerked back in surprise, but then his face split into a grin. "De Noronha. Fairbourne. What the devil are you two doing here?"

"Fairbourne?" Tiago cut his eyes to Gabe. "Since when are you called Fairbourne?"

"He just inherited his great-uncle's title," the duke explained. "Our humble lieutenant is now a viscount."

"You did not tell me this," Tiago said.

"It just happened," Gabe muttered. "I'll explain later."

"And I have to call you this, Fair… Fair… What was it again?"

"You can call me Davenport. It's fine."

"Good, because—"

"De Noronha!" the duke barked. "I believe I asked you a question."

Tiago quickly explained his reasons for being in England.

"What?" the duke snapped once Tiago came to the part about Nigel trying to strip Abbie of her portion. Having heard the rumors that the duke had a soft spot for a pretty face, Abbie batted her eyes, trying to look innocent and beleaguered.

It worked if the fire that came into the duke's eyes was any indication. "That swine! And what's worse, she is Captain Lord Hartlebury's sister. He must not get away with it!"

"I could not agree with you more, sir," Tiago said gravely.

The duke glanced at his pocket watch. "I have a half-hour to spare. Why don't I sit in on this hearing?"

Mr. Vickery responded to this suggestion with

predictable enthusiasm, and in short order, the six of them were seated around the defense table.

Abbie would relish the look of horror that crossed Nigel's face when he entered the hearing room for years to come. First, his eyes fell upon Tiago. She could almost mark the moment he placed his uniform as that of a *Portuguese* officer. A pallor swept across his face. Then he spied the Duke of Wellington seated at Abbie's side, and his face turned from white to green.

As he fumbled to pull out his chair, Abbie wondered if he might cast his accounts right there in the middle of the hearing room.

The corrupt Judge Waring re-entered the room from a side door, frowning when he noticed the duke sitting at the defense table. "Your Grace," he stuttered, "I-I thought your business had concluded."

"I find I have a material interest in this case," Wellington replied.

The judge fumbled his papers as he took his seat behind the pulpit. "May I enquire as to the nature of this interest?"

"I am here to serve as a character witness," the duke said firmly.

"Ch-character witness," Judge Waring said. "Just so. Well, shall we begin?"

Mr. Vickery smiled as he rose to his feet. "Let's."

CHAPTER 16

"**W**ell," Abbie said, "that exceeded all of my wildest hopes."

Their party, save the Duke of Wellington, who had to hurry off to another appointment, was gathered in the hall, savoring their victory. During the hearing, Mr. Vickery had presented the marriage contract Abbie found in the attic and had posited that it was the real reason Nigel had filed suit. Every time Nigel's barrister had tried to object—that it was unrelated to the current suit, that the matter had already been finalized, that there was no evidence that the contract Abbie had found was valid—the Duke of Wellington had contradicted him.

Not that the duke had any legal authority. But really—he was the *Duke of Wellington*. Failing to acquiesce to his opinion constituted both social and political suicide, and it seemed that neither Nigel nor Judge Waring had much stomach for it.

And Rodrigo de Noronha turned out to be a better witness than anyone could have hoped. Not only had he brought with him a sheaf of papers bearing Carlotta's true signature, demonstrating rather compellingly that the signature on Nigel's copy of the marriage contract had been forged, he had traveled with Carlotta to England and personally overseen her marriage settlement all those years ago. The true contract, Rodrigo testified, was the one Abbie had found, and Carlotta had returned to Portugal complaining bitterly that the Davies had cheated her.

Nigel's face took on a pinched quality as he sensed the writing on the wall. "My apologies, Mr. de Noronha. As this all took place years before my birth, I knew nothing of it."

Abbie was surprised the force of her glare didn't bore holes in his skull. Because, of course, that was a lie. Nigel had admitted that he knew Carlotta had been robbed.

But, as he offered to sign Carlotta's dowry back over to Rodrigo on the condition that the Dulson estate would not be asked to pay back the income it had generated over the past sixty years, and drop his suit against Abbie to boot, she chose to bite her tongue.

And when Mr. de Noronha, delighted to have the missing piece of his family's estate restored, insisted upon paying the legal fees and costs Abbie had incurred in defending the case, her happiness was complete.

Well, she thought, glancing up at Gabe.

Almost.

Mr. Vickery bowed over her hand. "I am delighted that you have finally attained the result you deserve, my lady." He consulted his pocket-watch. "I pray you will excuse me, but I have another hearing starting in ten minutes."

"Of course." Abbie squeezed his fingers where they held her own. "Thank you, Mr. Vickery. For everything."

"You are most welcome." He bowed once more before taking his leave.

Tiago and his grandfather had withdrawn a few paces and were having a hushed conversation on the far side of the hall. Abbie decided this was as good a time as any to confront Gabe.

She nudged him with her elbow. "Care to explain what Tiago was saying earlier?"

He swallowed thickly but said nothing.

"In spite of your earlier denials, he seems convinced that you're not indifferent to me." Summoning all of her nerve, she forced herself to add, "He even referred to me as the woman you love."

His eyes were mournful as he gazed down at her in the shadowy hall. "It doesn't change anything, Abbie."

Her heart flared with hope, even as he told her it was impossible. "But you do love me."

"Of course I do." His voice was gentle but held a note of despair. "At Salamanca, for one brief, shining moment, I thought Hart was asking *me* to marry you. And that was the moment I realized that I..." He tore his gaze from hers, swallowing thickly.

She took his gloved hand in both of hers and pressed it. "There has to be a way."

He wouldn't look at her. "There's not."

"There *has to*." Her voice cracked, and she paused to draw in a slow breath before continuing, "I don't care about leading a life of luxury. Let's run away together. To America. To Canada. To the ends of the earth, if that's the only place we can be together."

At least that shocked him into looking at her. "You can't mean that."

She felt tears welling in the corners of her eyes. "I do mean it. I don't care if we're poor. I don't care if I have to be a frontier wife. I'll learn to cook. I'll haul water. I'll sleep in a shanty." One of the tears escaped across her cheek, and she swiped at it with the back of her hand. "The only thing that matters is that I'm with you."

She felt his thumb caress the back of her hand, but his eyes remained sad. "I would do it without a single misgiving, had I not inherited this blasted title. But it's not just Great-aunt Matilda I have to look after. There are elderly servants who deserve a pension so they can live out their final years with dignity. Crofters whose cottages are falling apart around them. Tradesmen whose businesses will go under if I don't pay off my great-uncle's debts. I can't walk away, can't turn my back on them, no matter how much I wish I could."

Abbie nodded. Her tongue felt thick in her throat, but she managed to say, "And so what you need is an heiress."

"I'm so sorry, Abbie. If there was any other way—"

"How far is it to Lymington?" Tiago asked, causing both Abbie and Gabe to jerk in surprise. He cringed as he noted their drawn expressions and the way Gabe furtively withdrew his hand from Abbie's grasp. "Oh, dear—I can see that I have interrupted."

"It's all right," Abbie, said, waving one hand and fishing her handkerchief out of her reticule with the other. In the hearing room, she'd heard Gabe explaining his situation to Tiago in hushed whispers, so Tiago understood that there could be no happy ending to their story. "We were just finishing." She dabbed hastily at her eyes. "Lymington is about a hundred miles from London."

"Then we can make it there in one day," Tiago mused.

Abbie gave a startled laugh. "Only if you have an exceptionally fast conveyance."

Tiago grinned. "Which I do."

"Why do you want to go to Lymington, anyway?" Gabe asked.

"I believe you mentioned finding some of my great-aunt's effects in the dower house," Tiago said. "And she is also buried in Lymington, is she not?"

"You are correct on both counts," Abbie confirmed.

Tiago nodded solemnly. "Then I would like to retrieve her belongings and pay my respects at her grave. We will all need to gather a few things. Perhaps we can meet back here in one hour?"

"I'm not sure it will take an hour," Gabe said gruffly.

A gleam came into Tiago's eyes. "An hour. There is one last item of my Aunt Carlotta's business I need to take care of."

CHAPTER 17

The distance was long, but then, so were the days.
Mr. de Noronha preferred not to undertake such a
long journey, so it was Abbie, Gabe, and Tiago who set out
together in Tiago's hired carriage. Abbie had brought
Carlotta's journal to London, so they passed the time reading
her most amusing entries aloud and listening to Tiago's
favorite memories of his irreverent auntie.

They arrived in Lymington just as shades of orange and
gold started to streak the sky. Abbie directed the coachman
to St. Thomas's Church, then led Tiago to his great-aunt's
grave. He knelt upon the ground and began speaking softly
in Portuguese. Abbie and Gabe retreated to the graveled path
to allow him some privacy.

After a few minutes, Tiago nodded solemnly, then rose.
As he crossed the churchyard to rejoin Gabe and Abbie, he
had a soft smile on his face.

"It's a peaceful place, isn't it?" Abbie said. "I like to come
here sometimes and talk to Carlotta, too. You'll think me
silly, but I have come to think of her as a friend."

"I don't think you silly at all," Tiago said. "In fact, I am not surprised. I have a feeling, a very distinct feeling"—he pressed a hand to his heart—"that she thinks of you as her friend, too. It is why she approves so strongly of what I am about to do."

Abbie tilted her head to the side. "Whatever do you mean?"

Tiago's gaze was fixed on Gabe. "Did Davenport ever tell you about the time he saved my life?"

"No," Abbie replied.

Gabe waved this off. "I didn't, really. It was nothing."

"He saved my life," Tiago insisted, turning to Abbie. "It was during the Battle of Vitoria. My horse was shot out from under me, and I was trapped beneath him. I could see the French troops closing in. They say that before you die, your life flashes before your eyes. It is true. Suddenly, I saw my mother, and my father, and my three sisters. My older brothers, both of whom died before me. As well as my grandfather, and all my aunts and uncles and cousins. And I knew in that horrible moment that I would never see them again."

He gestured to Gabe. "But then, who should I see but my friend Davenport. He shot one French soldier and took out two more with his bayonet, all while shouting like a madman for his men to form ranks. He put himself between me and the enemy soldiers without a second's hesitation. Suddenly there was a wall of red-coats between me and the French line, and Davenport was pulling me out from beneath my horse."

Abbie glanced at Gabe. He looked distinctly surly at this recounting of his heroism. "It was nothing. Just doing my job."

"Hmm." Tiago looked distinctly skeptical of this claim, but he let it pass. "Well, you did a good job of it. I made it back home to my family." He turned to Abbie. "Do you believe in providence?"

Abbie paused to consider the question. "A year ago, I probably would have said no. After losing my parents, my brother, and my freedom in such short order, I didn't see much evidence of divine protection. But…"

"But?" Tiago prompted.

"But I felt something," Abbie said in a rush. "In the moment I found Carlotta's diary. I felt it before I opened the cover, before I even realized what it was. I know it sounds silly—"

"It doesn't," Tiago reassured her.

"But I feel like I was meant to find it. Like Carlotta has been watching over me. Like she is my very own guardian angel." She gave a weak chuckle. "I'm sure that sounds ridiculous."

"I do not think it sounds ridiculous at all," Tiago said. "You see, I, too, believe in providence. The only reason I am alive today is because Davenport saved my life at Vitoria. And the only reason I am standing here, happy to have recovered my family's legacy at long last, is because you had the moral strength to hold out against Nigel, even when it appeared that doing the right thing would bring about your own ruin."

A gleam came into Tiago's eyes. "Now, it happens that Carlotta's dowry did not merely consist of a piece of my family's vineyards. She also had three thousand pounds' worth of stock in the Bank of England, which was also restored to my family today. After the hearing concluded, my grandfather and I stopped in at the London bank that has been overseeing the investment to enquire as to how much it is worth today. Would you care to wager a guess?"

"It wouldn't surprise me if it's doubled in value," Gabe said.

Tiago laughed. "It has done better than double, because my great-grandfather, in his wisdom, specified that each year, half of the proceeds from the dividend were to be used to buy more stock. And after the passage of sixty-one years, I am pleased to report that this stock is now worth 61,779 pounds."

"Sixty-one thousand pounds!" Gabe exclaimed. Abbie studied his face in the fading light. He was blinking rapidly, and she knew he must be feeling at least a pang of jealousy, that his friend had received such an unexpected windfall, a windfall that Gabe himself so desperately needed. But if he felt bitter, he showed no sign of it. His eyes were sincere as he clapped Tiago on the shoulder and said, "That's brilliant. It really is. I'm happy for you."

"You may be happy for yourself because the money will be going to you."

Gabe blanched. "No, Tiago. What are you saying? It's too much."

"That is not for you to say, because we are not giving it to you. We're giving it to Abbie." Tiago's grin was smug. "Because this way, you have to marry her."

It was Abbie's turn to blanch. "Oh, my goodness! As grateful as I am, I could never accept such a gift."

"I have already discussed it with my grandfather," Tiago said. "It is decided." Gabe tried to say something, but Tiago cut him off, "And do not try to tell me it is too much. Too much for the man who saved my life, and the woman who risked everything to protect my family's legacy?" He huffed dismissively. "The money, it is not so important. Believe me, with our vineyard restored to its full glory, we will have plenty of money. This is the right thing. It is *providence*. And"—he nodded firmly toward his great-aunt's grave —"Carlotta agrees with me."

Abbie wrung her hands. "But—"

"No buts," Tiago said, claiming her hand and placing it upon his arm. He led her firmly to the foot of Carlotta's grave. "Come, stand here. You will understand."

Abbie tried to take a step back, but Tiago covered her hand where it rested upon his forearm, holding her in place. Her heart was flying and there was an unbearable tension in her breast like a violin string wound too tight.

"Breathe," Tiago whispered. "Listen."

The first thing she noticed was a faint breeze, caressing her temple. It was cooling.

Soothing.

And then, the strangest thing happened. The tightness in her chest slowly unfurled, like a rose opening to the summer sun. Her pulse slowed, and she took a gasping breath.

A feeling washed over her. It felt almost like… peace.

She opened her eyes to find Tiago watching her. "You feel it, too. Do you not?"

Abbie didn't quite trust herself to speak, but she gave a small nod.

"This is what Carlotta wants," Tiago insisted. "In a way, it makes sense. You are her rightful heir. Her fellow Lady Dulson."

That startled a laugh out of her.

Tiago smiled, encouraged. "You will accept the money, then?"

"I will." She caught a tear with the palm of her glove before it could progress across her cheek. "I—I don't know how to thank you."

"Ah, but I do." Tiago's eyes gleamed. "You can make my dear friend the happiest man in all of England."

They turned toward Gabe. He was waving his hands, palms out, as if that would deter Tiago one bit. His eyes were slightly wild, showing more white than green, and he couldn't seem to fix them on any one point. "That's grand of you, de Noronha. To give that to Abbie. I like the thought of her having that money. Of her being taken care of. But that doesn't mean that I…" He swallowed thickly, then tried again. "I—I just… I can't…"

"But you love her!" Tiago protested.

Gabe seemed to be looking everywhere but at Abbie. "I do. But I… I…"

"I know what this is," Tiago said. "This is about the promise her brother forced you to make at Salamanca. You have convinced yourself that you are not good enough for her. Haven't you?"

Gabe's cheeks were ruddy beneath his golden tan. "I'm *not* good enough for her. Leaving aside the fact that her own brother didn't think so, I come with fifty thousand pounds of debt. If a man in similar financial straits came sniffing after her, I would run him off without hesitation."

"And I would want you to," Abbie said, "if he were the type of man who had run up those debts at the gaming tables, or by purchasing diamond-encrusted snuffboxes. But you were not irresponsible. You inherited your situation through no fault of your own."

Gabe made a slashing motion with his hand. "Still, I won't allow you to be taken advantage of by some fortune hunter." He frowned. "Even when the fortune hunter is me."

Tiago shook his head. "Well, I have something to say about all of this. And it involves Abbie's brother. You see, a true friend does not stab you in the back." He held up a finger. "A true friend stabs you in the *front*."

"Or," Gabe said, "possibility number three—a true friend doesn't stab you at all."

Tiago dismissed this with a flick of his hand. "My point is, if you have something to say, you do not say it behind a man's back. No, I will say it directly to Hart."

"Notwithstanding the fact that he's dead," Gabe muttered.

Tiago ignored him. "He is buried here as well, yes, Abbie?"

"He is," Abbie confirmed. "This way."

She led the way to her brother's grave, which stood beside that of her parents. It was on the edge of the churchyard, near a little grove of trees. Her heart gave a familiar squeeze as she faced the fact that her entire family was on the other side of the soil, while she was here, alone in the world.

Tiago turned to Abbie. "I hope you will not take any offense at what I am about to say. I knew your brother for a short time before his death, and my impression was that he was a very good man. But we all have our weaknesses, our blind spots. I could tell that Hart sincerely loved Davenport and that he treasured his friendship. But"—Tiago turned to face Gabe—"he was accustomed to a certain dynamic in that friendship. He was used to being the leader, the one everyone looked up to. He was the viscount, while you did not have a title. He was rich, and you were not. Indeed, although you entered the army at the same time, by the time I met you, he was a captain and you were a mere lieutenant because he could afford to purchase a promotion, while you had to wait to receive one."

Gabe shifted uncomfortably. "Hart was a good friend to me. He never made me feel like I was less than him."

"Oh, to be sure!" Tiago exclaimed. "But in the back of his mind, I do believe he took it for granted that he was the leader. It was that way in just about every area. Except"—Tiago fixed Gabe with a meaningful look—"when it came to women."

Tiago turned to Abbie. "Now, I do not mean to make it sound like Davenport spent his time in the army chasing after skirts. I can attest to the fact that he did not. But he was the one who drew every female eye when he walked into a room. When it came to women, he was number one, and it was your brother who had to play second fiddle."

Gabe frowned. "What are you saying?"

"Hart was jealous," Tiago said. "We think of jealousy as such a low emotion. And I suppose it is, but it is a very human failing. I do not fault him for having those feelings. It seems that he knew they were unworthy, and mostly, he did not act on them." Tiago shook his head. "It is just unfortunate that, in the one moment he had a lapse, he did not have time to come around, to realize his mistake so he could apologize. Because I know there is no one he esteemed higher than you, Davenport. He thought of you already as his brother. I know he did. And if he could see you today, with clear eyes, see the way you esteem his sister, the way you care for her, then I know there is no one else he would want her to take for her husband."

Gabe couldn't seem to tear his eyes from Hart's grave. "I —I don't know."

He sounded unsure.

Unsure was an improvement upon *entirely unconvinced*, which is how he had sounded just a moment before.

Abbie walked up to Gabe and took his hand. "I think Tiago has the right of it." She turned to face her brother's grave. "I love you, Hart," she said, her voice shaking. "You're a mutton-headed fool for trying to scare Gabe away from me. But you're *my* mutton-headed fool, and I still think you were the best big brother in the world."

"Yes," Tiago said. "Good! Come, Davenport." He grabbed Gabe's shoulders and spun him so he was facing Hart's grave. "Now it's your turn."

CHAPTER 18

Gabe found it hard to even look at his best friend's grave. After nine years in the army, it wasn't as if he was a stranger to death.

But this was different. This was *Hart*.

Then there was the fact that he had broken his vow. Even though Abbie's arguments that it wasn't for Hart to dictate what happened to her rang true, Gabe found it was much easier to absolve himself of this sin from a hundred miles away in London than it was when he was standing at the foot of his best friend's grave.

Tiago squeezed his shoulders encouragingly. "Go ahead. Tell him."

"I feel like an idiot," Gabe muttered.

"Perhaps it would help if I gave you some privacy." Tiago retreated to the far side of the churchyard, then gestured for Gabe to proceed.

Gabe sighed as he turned back toward Hart's headstone. "Hart," he began, his voice sounding stilted to his own ears. What the hell was he supposed to say? "I—" He gave a huff of frustration. "I was going to say I was sorry I broke my pledge to you. But seeing as I'm standing in a churchyard, I probably shouldn't lie. I'm not sorry. I'm not sorry in the least."

He glanced at Abbie and found it was easier to speak when he was looking at her. "You see, I never should have promised that I wouldn't touch Abbie. I knew even then that I had fallen in love with her. That I wanted to spend the rest of my life with her. So I should have refused your request, even on your deathbed."

A tear slipped from the corner of Abbie's eye. She wiped it with the heel of her hand before it could streak across her cheek.

But there was adoration in her eyes, mingled with the sadness, and that gave him the strength to soldier on. "I know I'm not the man you wanted for your sister. But I'll make you a new promise today, one I'll never regret. I promise to love Abbie, to be faithful to her, and to cherish her always. I promise that I will be everything you could ever want her to have in a husband."

There was no sound in the churchyard save for the rustling of the wind in the trees.

"That's all," Gabe muttered. "Other than..." He still felt absurd, but as long as he was doing this, he might as well go the whole hog.

He drew in a ragged breath and forced the words out before he had time to think better of them. "I love you, too, Hart. I love you like you were my own brother. And I miss you every day. Even if Abbie is right, and you could sometimes be a nog-headed arse."

He fell silent. He and Abbie both had their heads bowed.

After a moment, Abbie squeezed his hand. Her eyes were bright. "That was good. Really good." She tilted her head toward the spot where Tiago awaited them. "Come. It's time to go."

Gabe nodded. He gave one last mournful look at his best

friend's grave. Now that he had his own estate to attend to, who knew when he would find himself back this way?

But even if he couldn't visit much in person, he would never forget. He would carry every happy memory he and Hart had ever had with him.

Always.

They had scarcely reached the graveled path when a rustling sound came from the grove of trees behind them.

Gabe glanced over his shoulder.

Beside him, Abbie gasped.

A stag stepped out of the woods. Gabe had never seen such a magnificent specimen. It was huge, its antlers easily three feet long, and its russet coat thick and glossy.

Gabe expected the stag to flee at the sight of them, but much to his astonishment, it strode calmly, majestically, across the path and onto the green, unperturbed by the pair of humans a mere fifteen feet away.

It finally came to a stop just beside Hart's headstone.

Hart. Suddenly Gabe's heart was pounding out of his chest.

"Gabe," Abbie whispered, "it's—"

"A hart," he finished for her, his voice strangled. They were clinging to each other's hands, and… Gabe didn't know what to think. It was ridiculous. It was *impossible.*

A *hart* was standing on his best friend, Hart's, grave, as tranquil as the surface of a pond. It sounded like some childish fancy to regard it as a sign. And yet even Gabe, hardened soldier that he was, couldn't help but wonder…

The hart stood perfectly still, regarding them with serene brown eyes. An image flashed through his mind of Hart's warm brown eyes, crinkling at the corners as he smiled. It looked at Abbie, and then at Gabe.

Then slowly, deliberately, it bowed its head.

It held the pose for sixteen beats of Gabe's thundering

heart before it straightened. Then it strode back across the green and disappeared into the woods, leaving not a trace behind.

Abbie and Gabe stood in stunned silence, clinging to each other. Eventually, Abbie shook her head. "Did I imagine that?"

"If you did, we're sharing the same delusion." Gabe ran a hand over his eyes. "I can't believe I'm about to say this."

What an understatement. Gabe didn't believe in this rot. He'd spent nine years in the army. He'd fought in all the bloodiest battles—Albuera, Talavera, Waterloo. He'd buried far too many of his friends to believe in guardian angels.

If Gabe had a guardian angel, he'd done a shit job for the first thirty-one years of his life.

And yet… and yet… what other explanation was there for that hart?

He had nothing. And he suddenly realized that deep down…

… he *wanted* to believe. That your life wasn't just chance. That there was something else out there, some purpose to it all.

That the people he'd lost weren't really gone forever. That he would see Hart again, and his parents, too.

Someday.

Something inside of him shifted. When he glanced down at Abbie, he wasn't quite as jaded as he'd been the moment before. "I think your brother just gave us his blessing."

The strangest thing was, he actually meant it.

Tears were pouring down Abbie's face. "I think so, too."

Gabe fished his handkerchief out of his pocket. Gravel scattered as Tiago came skidding to a stop behind them. "You have to marry her now!"

Gabe laughed at his friend's mulish expression. "I'd already decided I would. But now…" He glanced toward the copse into which the hart had disappeared. "Now I won't feel guilty about it."

Tiago smiled, delighted. "So you have already proposed!"

"God damn it," Gabe muttered. "I didn't actually ask the question."

Abbie squeezed his arm. "The answer is yes."

Gabe studied her in the fading light. "Are you sure, Abbie? Let's face it, I'm a bit of a wreck. I didn't have the best childhood, and I just spent nine years in the army. I feel like you deserve someone better than me. Someone who's… whole."

Her eyes were bright. "What a coincidence. I'm broken, too. It's why we understand each other so well."

Gabe rubbed the back of his head. "I suppose that's true."

"We'll prop each other up," Abbie said. "We'll do well together. Better than if we were apart."

"A thousand times better," he agreed.

She tugged at his arm. "Come on. Let's go and be wrecks together."

Gabe nodded, his throat constricting. "I would like that."

Tiago was frowning as he fell into step beside them. "This is how you English propose?"

He caught Abbie's eye. One corner of her mouth curled up into a grin.

"Apparently it is," Gabe said.

They were both laughing as they strode forward together, into the future.

In the end, Abbie joined the Wicked Widows' League.

But only for one day.

They got back to London on a Wednesday. On Thursday, Rodrigo de Noronha transferred the Bank of England stock that had once belonged to Carlotta into Abbie's name. She used a small portion of her newfound fortune to properly pay her dues to the organization that had taken her in during her hour of distress.

And on Friday, she officially relinquished her status as a Wicked Widow by marrying Gabe by special license in the burgundy and cream parlor of Matron Manor.

All the widows attended, along with Mr. Vickery and some of Gabe's friends from the army. Gabe's Great-aunt Matilda swooned onto a settee upon learning that the ceremony was to take place at such a scandalous organization as the Wicked Widows' League and forcefully declined the invitation.

But that was all right. If Nigel and Uncle Edmond had

taught Abbie one thing, it was that blood wasn't always thicker than water.

The people who truly mattered were the ones who stood by you in your darkest hour. As far as she was concerned, she was surrounded by her real family on her wedding day.

Gabe recruited the army chaplain who had served with his unit to officiate. Tiago—in whom the widows took a great interest—stood up with Gabe, and Mr. de Noronha gave away the bride.

Gabe and Abbie promised to visit the de Noronha estate in Portugal someday. Tiago promised to serve as godfather to Gabe and Abbie's first child.

Lady Sylvan promised to slip a piece of ice down the back of Great-aunt Matilda's dress at the first opportunity.

After a lavish wedding breakfast, Abbie found herself in a familiar place: bouncing along in the back of a carriage with Gabe. Only this time, instead of black, she wore pink, and the filmy fabric obscuring her face wasn't a shroud, but a wedding veil.

Gabe gave her his scoundrel's smile. "I have a surprise for you, Lady Fairbourne."

"Lady Fairbourne!" Everything had happened so quickly, Abbie hadn't had time to consider her new title. "What an immense improvement over Lady Dulson."

He kissed the back of her hand. "I hope that I am likewise an improvement over Lord Dulson."

"The improvement is so vast it is inexpressible." Abbie started as she noticed grassy fields outside the carriage window. "Wait, is that Green Park? This isn't the way to Fairbourne House." She turned to find Gabe smiling mysteriously. "Where are we going?"

"There's only one place to go when you have purchased yourself a scoundrel, and that is the Pulteney Hotel. After all, you don't really want to spend your wedding night under the same roof as Aunt Matilda, do you?"

Abbie laughed. "I must say, I do not." She pretended to straighten the gold braid on his coat, as it gave her an excuse to touch him. "Conveniently, this heiress didn't merely come with sixty-one thousand pounds. I am also in possession of a lovely dowager cottage. Perhaps we should offer it to the dowager Lady Fairbourne."

"That is an excellent suggestion."

Abbie looped her arms around Gabe's neck and sifted her hands through the soft hair at his nape. "But in all seriousness, Gabe, I wish you wouldn't refer to yourself as something I *purchased*. I know they officially transferred the money into my name. But the de Noronhas intended it for both of us."

Gabe scooped her up into his lap. "By this time tomorrow, you'll have changed your mind."

She shook her head tightly. "I won't."

He trailed his fingertips down the length of her neck. "You bought me once. You've already seen what you get for a thousand pounds." He replaced his fingers with his lips, making Abbie gasp as goosebumps raced down her spine.

Gabe's voice was husky as he whispered in her ear, "Can you even imagine what you're going to get for sixty-one thousand?"

"I'm sure I cannot," Abbie said, her breath coming in pants as she threaded her fingers into his hair. "But I very much look forward to finding out."

They did not finish their debate, as there was no more conversation for some time hence.

But I can assure you, gentle reader, that Abbie never regretted her purchase.

~

KEEP READING for a special preview of the next book in the Wicked Widows' League series, *Scandalizing the Scoundrel* by Charlie Lane!

WOULD you like to see how Gabe and Abigail are doing a few years after their wedding? Subscribers to my newsletter will receive a free second epilogue short story so you can check in on their happily-ever-after! I'll give you a hint… Abbie decides to follow through on her suggestion that she tie Gabe to the bed! Visit www.courtneymccaskill.com if you'd like to sign up.

PREVIEW: SCANDALIZING THE SCOUNDREL

In this sizzling Regency romance novella by USA Today Bestselling author Charlie Lane, opposites attract as a shy widow and the scoundrel who loves her discover that passion is just the beginning and sometimes an affair isn't nearly enough.

A shy widow and a notorious scoundrel. She wants an affair, but he wants her heart.

Lady Fredericka has been quiet too long. She's ready to step out of the shadows of widowhood and into the spotlight of pleasure. Without risking her heart. Circus star and equestrian Grant Webster offers the delectable solution. Strong, handsome, and a flirtatious scoundrel, he'll warm her bed without asking for more. After all, a man like him would never seriously desire a quiet widow like her.

Grant has always commanded the adoration of the ladies. But since meeting the quietly lovely Lady Fredericka, he only wants her. When she suggests an affair, he's tempted … but refuses. His heart is too involved to give her the steamy flirtation she desires.

But Lady Fredericka won't give up.

And Grant can only be tempted so far.

When he finally gives in to passion, he becomes the seducer, tempting her to risk the pain of loss for a home of the heart with a man who loves her.

~

Chapter One

April 1822

When a man rode a horse like it was an extension of his own body, he likely managed other … *physical activity* with such skill. One of the many reasons Freddy had decided to make London's Golden Boy, the expert equestrian riding round the ring below, her paramour. She desired a skilled lover, and a vigorous one, and he promised much without saying a word.

He could hardly speak now, could he? Standing atop the giant horse, balancing as it took him in circles round Garrison's Circus's amphitheatre. Those in the audience attracted to his mesmerizing golden glitter leaned closer, breath held tight in their lungs, attuned to his every move and muscle flex.

Mr. Grant Webster entranced them all, and Freddy wanted more than silent promises. She wanted to be seduced. To do the seducing. Whichever, as long as her naked body laid alongside his at some point in the process.

She put a palm to her cheek. Was it burning as bright as it felt? And with her inconveniently pale coloring, anyone nearby would know the direction of her thoughts. She pulled her cloak tighter, to hide her blush, and backed away from the banister. She'd seen his act many times and did not need to stay until the end to know how it went. She did, however, need to get to the courtyard behind the amphitheatre. She had a plan based entirely on hearsay, whispers, and rumors that claimed Mr. Webster took a lady back to his dressing room each night, choosing whatever woman had snuck back there to be with him first.

Tonight, that lady would be Freddy. Because at five and thirty years of age, mother of two delightful daughters, and a widow for nearly four years, Freddy found herself missing the touch of a man.

Not just missing. Craving. Ever since that stolen moment away from Max and Nora's wedding breakfast. The man had brought her wine and cake and paid an unknown price for his kindness—her unwavering esteem.

He'd done nothing to damage her respect from that moment on, winking at her and joking with the girls when he came to dinner at Max's bidding. He often asked about her knitting with a hint of trepidation and an ocean of support. The poor man seemed to believe she'd ever improve in that area. And all that playful charm and kindness made him a ghost in her waking and sleeping life. He haunted her dreams and winked at her as she pleasured herself between her lonely sheets each night. But tonight, she meant to turn vision into reality.

Impossible to believe the man she meant to take as a lover was the one in the amphitheatre mesmerizing half of London. His very brightness should have scared her off, but her desire had grown too strong, an out-of-control need she could no longer ignore, crafted not only of physical attraction but of all those little moments, too—the wine and cake, the winks and jokes, unexpected kindness. He was a star, but he was also a man who offered her comfort. The perfect man to be her lover.

And the wise words of the *Wicked Widows* had led her one conclusion: she could make a willing lover of a scoundrel.

She could try at least.

Once away from the audience, she fled down the stairs and out the front doors. The night air was warm for an April evening, and clouds, gray and heavy, rolled across the sky, threatening a spring storm. She ran around the building and found a wrought iron gate. Well. She'd not expected that. Was it locked? Dread made her fingers heavy as mud as she reached out and explored. What would she do if the gate proved an affective barrier between herself and the one desire that had taken hold of her recently, refused to let her go until she did something about it?

She'd not considered locked gates while she'd crafted her plan to become bold enough to take a lover.

First, she'd meant to become good at her hobby—knitting. A failure there. She still missed more stitches than she made, but she'd discovered something useful. She enjoyed it and didn't care if she was good or not. That little revelation had been oddly freeing. She could do something entirely for herself without pressure of performing well.

She'd then moved on in her plan to scandalous reading material. She'd devoured Henry Fielding's *Tom Jones*. She didn't quite see why people were so bothered by it. But reading a book others gasped at while she enjoyed had given her a bit of courage to do other so-called naughty things. To try something, in fact, that was entirely scandalous. And a bit mad perhaps, too.

She'd run down the street and back. In the dark hours of

the nighttime morning. In nothing but her shoes and shift. She glowed red just thinking of it, felt alive, too. Even now, three months later. It had done the trick, certainly, let her know she was on the right track, the bold track that led to a lover.

Fourth, she'd begun to speak up for herself more often. Or tried to, especially when in large groups where she usually sank into her habitual invisibility. She'd attended many Cavendish dinners and said a word or two. Perhaps three. And not been ignored, either. *That* had felt lovely. To be heard.

Everything she'd done in service to this last goal, all meant to give her the courage to slip into that courtyard and take London's famous lover as her own.

If the cursed gate was not locked.

It was the final task on her list, so locked gate or no, she'd find a way. She had to. Her body ached with loneliness and need. Her heart did, too, but she'd ignore that particular organ because the *Widows* warned against its involvement and so did her experience. The love her heart desired would only come with the possibility of the pain of loss. Through death or disinterest, men left women's hearts hollow. Little girls' hearts too, daughters wailing for their papas in the middle of the night.

Freddy pressed her eyes tightly closed, snapping a gate closed against the memory and wrapping her hands tighter round the actual steel gate before her. With the smooth iron under her fingers, she found well-oiled hinges and a locking mechanism. She worked it and pushed, and the gate swung open. Not locked after all. All that worry for naught. Relief swooshed through her with the swoosh of air caused by the opening barrier. Nothing kept her from her goal. Nothing kept her from Mr. Webster. Except, perhaps, the jumbled mess of emotions tempting her to run. Except that little voice in her gut insisting she was not yet ready for such a giant leap, not yet ready to claim the title of wicked widow.

Why did she worry? She was taking a lover, not a husband. Husbands were the true threat.

Marriage could leave her a widow twice over, a fate she refused to meet, for her own sanity and for her daughters'. Besides, she did not need a husband to tell her what to do, to close his ears when she tried to speak up, to hush her voice and shadow over her like an oak tree over a strangled flower at its roots.

No. Lovers were much preferable, from her point of view —and according to *The Wicked Widows Guide.* And what better lover than the master equestrian? Handsome, charming, silly. He had flirted with her many times before. He'd brought her cake. Hopefully he'd not mind gifting her other delectable things.

She closed the gate gently behind her, and the iron kissed together silently, the gate and its frame nestled close and locked tight like lovers. The courtyard spread before her, a giant ring at the back of the building. If there had ever been any grass, it had long since been pounded to dust by horse hooves, tumblers, contortionists, and children playing. Mews stood to one side and the amphitheatre to the other. A single door was cut into the building's marble façade.

She strolled across the courtyard toward it. Surely his act was over or close to it. She bit her bottom lip, straightened her cloak, breathed into her cupped palm to make sure her breath still had a hint of the mint leaf she had chewed on earlier. The cloak had likely mussed her hair a bit, but that was good. Mussed hair gave a man thoughts of the bedroom, and that was where she wished to drag him. Or for him to drag her.

Either way was perfectly acceptable. Though, it should likely be him. In case she lost the nerve.

The door flung open, and almost hit her in the nose. She dodged out of its trajectory.

Come on, Freddy, don't be such a fool. She straightened herself and looked about for whomever had opened the door. Could it be … Ah. No. It was not Mr. Webster but a woman, someone Freddy did not know, garbed in spangles— a performer. If she stayed much longer, she'd be audience, too. To a kiss.

Could Freddy *do this* in front of others? Surely Mr. Webster's fellow performers were used to the sight of him kissing strange women in the courtyard, but Freddy had never kissed in front of a single other soul beside the soul of the man kissing her. Perhaps the kissing would wait until they reached his dressing room.

Her feet tapped to turn around and flee, but she planted them to the dust and refused to let them do as they wished.

The woman disappeared into the alleyway beyond the iron gate, and then the door opened again.

Freddy flung herself to the side as a man strode out of the building. Even without a moon high above, his hair glinted like golden threads. Too long and tied back in a short queue low on his neck, strands escaped to fall over his forehead and muddle with the perspiration there.

Mr. Grant Webster.

Knitting needles like knives, she wanted to lick that neck more than she wanted her next breath. She felt intoxicated by the sight of it, tendrils of lust wrapping round her every vein and tightening. She'd never felt such pulsing need. Was it just him or that she was doing something for herself? Something illicit that spoke to her every hidden and silence desire? If it was the latter, she'd better *do something,* then.

She rolled off the wall and launched herself at him, flung her arms about that very sweaty neck and pressed her lips to his. He startled, pushed back, peered into the shadows of her hood. "A strange maiden approaches. What shall I do with her? Hm. Eager hands. Welcome lips. I think I should kiss her."

She opened her mouth to say "yes please" but found the two tremulous words swept into the patient fury of his kiss, into the warm hollow of his mouth. She didn't need those words after all.

The kiss unfurled like the thin, streaky clouds floating across the moon. They promised rain, but the kiss promised a thunderstorm.

He spun them and walked her backward until her back hit the wall. "Eager, love?" He placed a palm on either side of her head and leaned over her, his body casting her in further shadow.

She nodded, stroked her fingertips down his muscular back. He wore only a waistcoat and shirtsleeves as he did in every performance to better show off his musculature. To give him better ease of movement also on his horse she assumed. It also gave her greater access to him. No wool to hide his warmth and strength from her.

The kiss was slow, meandering, like sipping tea in a garden at morning when the dew still clings to each petal and leaf. Yet it promised to grow, too, and singe her as the rising sun eviscerates the dew.

In the surge of feeling, she remembered how to kiss, how she'd been kissed with passion by her husband before she'd been forgotten. So she outlined his bottom lip with the tip of her tongue, and he opened dutifully for her. They deepened the kiss at the same time, exploring, reveling. He didn't touch her except with his lips, and the absence of his hands where she most wanted them—everywhere on her—seemed to heighten her pleasure, and as her pleasure increased, so too did her desire. She wanted more, *needed* it.

She fisted her hands in his cravat and broke away from the kiss. A momentary gathering of breath before diving back in. They were disparate heights, and as she turned her face up to him, her nose brushed the bottom of his cravat, and she spied the gold-and-diamond pin nestled in the folds, glinting in the moonlight. The bit of jewelry was like him—beautiful, sharp, and a bit unexpected. Paste or real? It did not matter. It shone exquisite all the same. Like him.

His hand appeared, a heavy, delicious weight on her cheek, and he stroked his fingers into her hair over her ear, taking the hood of her cloak with him.

Mesmerized by the winking gem in his cravat, by the earthy scent of the man she'd dreamed of for months now, she barely noticed but to lean into the caress.

The moon caught her face.

"Damn me." Mr. Webster jumped away from her. "Freddy?"

Freddy never cursed, but a *damn* might be appropriate. So many emotions laced his few words, chief among them shock. She straightened off the wall and smoothed her skirts. What to do with his shock? And was that a touch of disgust in his voice? Surely not. Please God, no.

He paced away from her, raking his hands through his hair. When he returned to stand before her, he said, "It *is* you. I had hoped I imagined it."

Hoped he'd imagined it? Well. Freddy pulled her cloak up over her head and tried to find her courage. She looked up to the heavens for help. The clouds had rolled away, and the stars winked hello, but their blinking seemed like laughter. Freddy cut her gaze away, gripped her hands before her.

Mr. Webster wrung his hands. "Good God, Freddy, I'm so sorry. I am so very, very sorry. I do beg your pardon, a thousand times over. I thought you someone else." He groaned, hunched his body to the left and dropped his face in his hands. "Max is going to kill me. The strongman is going to snap every bone in my body with his bare hands."

She held a hand out with a halting step toward him. "Do not worry, Mr. Webster. I will not tell my cousin."

"Well, that makes it a bit better. Man's a boxer and a viscount and married into the Cavendish family. If anyone can snap my bones, *and* my reputation, it's him. And if there existed any reason for him to do so, it's this."

She shook her head but lost the words to contradict him.

"Are you here to see him?" Mr. Webster asked.

"No. No … ah, I'm … here to see you." The last three words were spoken so low, Freddy barely heard them herself. She should not have said them. Why had she said them? They were pointless now. Now that she knew how little he thought of her, how mortified he was to have kissed her. The man loved every woman in London.

But for her. She rolled her lips between her teeth, clenched her tears tight to her chest, and strode around him toward the iron gate. Someone had left it open, and it banged against the fence. Thank goodness. The echoing clang might cover up the brittle breaking of her heart.

"Freddy!" Footsteps pounding after her across the dust. "Wait a moment."

She stopped, unable to do otherwise.

He ran around her and stopped between her and the gate. "You said you were looking for me? I know you likely wish to put a bullet through my heart right now. For kissing you. But if there is anything I can do for you, please say the word."

Anything.

Except kiss her, it seemed.

She had to offer some response though because her dazed and defeated brain had told him one truth—she was there to see him. She would not tell him the other truth. *Why* she was there to see him. But what, then?

She didn't dare look to the stars again, mocking things. And the dust had no answers. Neither did the iron bars behind him. She finally managed to meet his gaze but found nothing there but dark eyes, kind and gentle.

A bashful smile, half grown, greeted her. "How are your daughters? Last I visited Max, they were aching to learn to ride. Has Max purchased a horse yet for them?"

"No. No horse, but …" A way out of this muck. She swallowed to wet the way for words. "That is precisely why I came to see you. I was in the audience tonight, and I realized there is no better rider in all of London. England. The world!" She was laying it on a bit thick, but the words would come now without her prior approval. "I would … I know it is too much to ask, but … would *you*, perchance, give the girls riding lessons?"

He scratched his jaw, clean-shaven and strong. "I cannot."

"Oh." Further disappointment? Or relief? A mix of both, no doubt.

"I am busy."

"Ah. Of course." She shook her head and stepped around him. "I am sorry to waste your time." She wrapped her fingers around the gate, cold and unforgiving, and slipped through.

She tripped, the back of her gown catching snug on some metal. She turned to release herself and found the skirts not trapped on some iron spear, but between the strong fingers of the trick rider. He stepped closer to her, his hand dark against the pale-green muslin of her gown, his gaze fixed to the meeting point of her skirts and his skin.

He dropped the material like a hot coal and darted his

gaze to her face. His eyes held stars in their dark-brown depths, and they found her lips and seemed unable to look away.

"I"—he cleared his throat, stepped even closer so that she could smell the horse and sweat on him again—"I do apologize. You are a lady and do not deserve such treatment, especially from the likes of me. Do … do you need an escort home?"

She shook her head. "I have borrowed the Cavendish carriage this evening." Max's in-laws were well-to-do and generous. She had use of the conveyance whenever she pleased. "I am well taken care of."

He ripped his gaze from her lips. "Of course. Good." A weak smile. "I'll help you find it, shall I?"

She needed time to think, but she could not seem to tell him no, so they stepped into the alley together and right into a warm body.

A small feminine scream emitted as the body tumbled to the ground.

"Bloody hell. How many other women will I assault this evening?" Mr. Webster squatted before the shadowy lump. "Are you hurt, madame?"

"I do not think so." A sultry voice. The woman lifted her face to Mr. Webster and the moonlight. No hiding for this woman. Young and beautiful and golden, she had no need of shadows. "Can you help me to my feet, Mr. Webster?"

He did, and she clung to his arm.

"My, you're as strong as you look. I was so hoping to … speak with you this evening. Shall we retire to your dressing room for a *conversation*?"

Freddy slipped through the alley, leaving the conversation behind her.

Mr. Webster did not call her back, had likely not even noticed she'd left.

A spin-off of the Cavendish Family series, this Wicked Widows novella is a low-angst stand-alone with plenty of laughs and heat. Order your copy of *Scandalizing the Scoundrel* today!

HISTORICAL NOTE

There were two areas where I bent the historical record for the sake of simplicity, so please consider this to be my mea culpa:

- There were many points in history in which the number of would-be army officers far exceeded the number of available promotions, and a man could get stuck in the position of lieutenant for nine years, as happens to Gabe. The Peninsular War, however, was not one of those periods. In actuality, the casualty rate was so high that officers advanced through the ranks fairly rapidly and there was no need to purchase a commission unless one wanted a place in one of the most fashionable regiments. A man like Gabe who started as a lieutenant and survived nine years of service would likely have received several promotions. Because I already had one name change planned for Gabe during the course of the story, from Lieutenant Davenport to Lord

Fairbourne, I decided to hold his army rank steady in order to minimize confusion.

- Lymington is indeed about a hundred miles from London, but it would have been a very fast carriage indeed that could have made the trip in one day! Although not entirely impossible, it would have been a very long and uncomfortable day and they would likely have stopped overnight. As the story was driving toward its climax, I decided to assume the weather was fair, the horses fast, and the road conditions perfect so they could make it in one.

ABOUT THE AUTHOR

After reading *Black Beauty* for the 1,497[th] time, Courtney McCaskill was inspired to write her own stories. Reviews of her early work were mixed, with her fourth-grade teacher, Mrs. Compton, saying, "Please stop writing all of your essays from the point of view of a horse."

Today, Courtney lives in Austin, Texas with the hero of her own story, who holds the distinction of being the world's most sarcastic pediatrician. She is reliably informed by her son that she gives THE BEST hugs, "because you're so squishy, Mommy." When she's not busy almost burning her house down while attempting to make a traditional Christmas pudding, she enjoys playing the piano, learning everything there is to know about Kodiak bears, and of course, curling up with a great book. Visit her online at www.courtneymccaskill.com.

ACKNOWLEDGMENTS

I would like to thank Dawn Brower for including me in this set and Tracy Sumner for putting in a good word for me. Thanks also to my wonderful editor, Diana Bold; my beta reader, Linda, for helping me purge those pesky Americanisms; and Amanda Mariel for making such a gorgeous cover for my book. I'd also like to give a shout-out to all of my writing buddies, especially my fellow Brazen Belles, everyone in Regency Fiction Writers, and my Romancestagram Fam!

The biggest thank-you of all goes to my wonderful family. Victor, this one's for you!